Sh[illegible]elf

"It's [illegible] whispered as she lifted Monk's hand to her lips and nibbled gently on his fingertips.

"I think it's like riding a bicycle." Monk's voice thickened. "Once you learn how, you always know."

The hoarseness in his voice had a strange effect on Phoebe's knees. She leaned against him and his arms swept around her, taking advantage of her weakness. "I want to make love with you," he murmured as he covered her mouth with the hot, sweet fire of his.

Phoebe pressed closer and her shyness fled as Monk's hands enflamed her. "No more waiting," she said huskily. "Love me, love me now."

"The pleasure," he breathed, "will be all mine. . . ."

For the group who helped me
unfold the story of Phoebe's jester.

LEIGH ROBERTS
is also the author
of this title in
Temptation

SIREN SONG

Head Over Heels

LEIGH ROBERTS

MILLS & BOON LIMITED
15–16 BROOK'S MEWS
LONDON W1A 1DR

First published in Great Britain in 1987 by Mills & Boon Limited, 15–16 Brook's Mews, London W1A 1DR

ISBN 0 263 75683 1

21–0387

Printed and bound in Great Britain by Cox & Wyman Ltd, Reading

1

THE MUSIC POUNDED and surged relentlessly. Phoebe Sullivan felt marooned in an ocean of supple leotard-encased bodies, all bending and stretching in unison, all sleek with perspiration. Once again she stumbled. Her friend Angie Molinaro put out a hand to steady her.

"Look out!" Angie hissed, her face glistening. She had had the forethought to tug on a headband that caught the sweat before it could drip into her eyes.

Wiping her own face on her sleeve, Phoebe wished fervently that she were somewhere—anywhere—else. This was no way to spend a lovely spring morning. "It's my shoes," she muttered to Angie. "The carpet in here seems to grab them somehow. . . ."

There was no time for explanation. All those well-toned bodies had somehow formed a line, a line that was rapidly bearing down on her.

"Weave left!" The instructor had to use considerable lung power to be heard above the music. Thankfully Phoebe watched the line move smartly away from her. "Weave right!" Now they were coming back again. Desperate to get out of the way, she wrapped one leg around the other, trying to copy what the others were doing. Her feet would have none of it.

"Step-kick!" Thank God! That was one movement she had mastered, except for the sly way the soles of her ancient tennis shoes caught on the carpet. It was better if she barely moved her feet—better for her shoes and for her pounding heart, which almost outpaced the music.

"Remember to work at your own pace." The instructor's words sounded unexpectedly close, causing her treacherous feet to do her in once again. This time she would have fallen if he hadn't caught her just in time.

She hadn't felt so inept, so embarrassed, since the long-ago torments of high school. Slowly she let her eyes travel from the hand on her arm up to a tanned, muscular shoulder. He was wearing a sweat-soaked tank top with a No Bozos graphic printed on the front. Standard-issue gray sweatpants covered his lean hips and legs. As the music ended, she forced her gaze to his face.

He wasn't too tall, she noted—an inch or two shy of six feet. He looked to be in his mid-thirties, with a clever, sun-browned face and dark hair that was cut short in front, although she saw in inexplicable detail that it curled down a bit on his neck. His eyes were the most startling blue she'd ever seen in real life—crystalline, sparkling, vibrantly alive. Paul Newman eyes, she told herself dreamily.

He was still grasping her by the arm, she realized, and with a blush of mortification she pulled away. "Thanks," she mumbled. He urged her into a walk, circling the big room at the health club as the other members of the aerobic dance class were doing, their fingers on their pulse points, their eyes fixed on a large clock at the front of the room.

"Time to take your pulse," the instructor said. She liked his voice, vibrant with a husky quality that reached deep inside her. "Do you know how?"

She put her fingers on her wrist, but he shook his head. "Like this," he told her, taking her hand and guiding it to her neck where the artery throbbed heavily. "Count it for ten seconds and see how it stacks up against your target heart rate on that chart under the clock."

He walked beside her while she tried to count her pulse and watch the clock. "It's hard if you're not used to it," he said, taking in the confused shake of her head. "This is your first time, isn't it?"

Nodding, she repressed a smile. Life was full of little virginities, she knew. But some of them were more absurd than others, and this, for her, was the most absurd of all. She was martyring her flesh and sacrificing her pride for the sake of a man whom she hadn't seen in years—the man who had been the recipient of her most important virginity.

"Let me help you," the instructor said. The amazing blue eyes showed nothing but friendly concern. Phoebe gulped when his warm hand slid around her neck to find the pulse point. "Hold still for a minute," he ordered. Obediently she stopped. The music began again, and the regular members of the class started jogging, some of them streaming out the door to brave the chill Missouri spring weather.

It was a good thing, she thought hazily, that her pulse was already racing. Otherwise she might have been afraid that the touch of this man's hand would make it jump, that he would know—what? That she was unused to a man's touch?

Angie halted beside them, jogging in place, her shiny black curls bouncing around her shoulders. Phoebe glanced enviously at her friend's trim body, clad in a lavender leotard that left nothing to the imagination. Angie was a regular in this class; she had insisted that exercise was the way out of Phoebe's dilemma.

"How's it going, Phoebe?" She batted her long black eyelashes at the instructor as he finished counting Phoebe's pulse. "You're new, aren't you? I haven't seen you teach this class before."

The man's crooked smile revealed white teeth and crinkled up the corners of those astounding eyes. He wasn't really good looking, Phoebe decided, trying to assess him the way Angie always sized up men. He wasn't tall enough to be a hunk, and he was faintly snub nosed. But when he smiled, the creases in his face somehow seemed to arrange themselves around his eyes in a very devastating manner.

"I'm filling in for Ross today," he explained. Ross Belden, Angie had told her, was the owner of the Fitness Emporium, the finest body shop in Kirkwood, Missouri. "You a member of the club?" The instructor's eyes ran over Angie in a detached appraisal.

Angie nodded, smiling, but he turned back to Phoebe without picking up on Angie's rather blatant invitation. "Don't overdo. Your pulse was a little high. Try to keep it below one hundred fifty. If you need to stop to take it, by all means do. No reason to kill yourself."

Phoebe nodded at these instructions. When the man turned away, she seized the opportunity to retie the drawstring of her new navy sweatpants. Navy was much more slimming than gray. She hadn't been able to find any black ones.

Class members returned to the room when the jogging song ended, lining up for more aerobic dancing. Would it never end? Doggedly Phoebe shuffled, kicked, jumped, bounced and swayed, wishing it were over, wishing she knew where the bathroom was.

Looking around at the others, who seemed to be performing effortlessly the most intricate and exhausting maneuvers, she groaned as she imagined the figure she must cut. Of the twenty-or-so people in the room, she was the only one—besides the instructor—in plain old sweatpants. Everyone else had some kind of form-fitting, figure-revealing, color-coordinated exercise outfit that showed off a shapely body. There were several men in the class, their attire as brief and provocative as the women's.

But what really made her cringe had little to do with clothes. Of all the people in the room, she was the only one who was thirty pounds overweight.

Finally the pace of the music slowed, and the dancers walked about the room, swinging their arms, stretching to cool down. Phoebe drew the first relaxed breath that she had taken in the past half-hour, though the sweat was still breaking out on her body faster than she could wipe it away.

Angie walked beside her, greeting friends in the class and filling Phoebe in on their private lives. "That's John," she said, nodding at a handsome blonde who appeared to have energy to spare, despite exertions that had left Phoebe weak in the knees. "He's really into the Nautilus equipment. I think he enters Mr. America contests and stuff."

"He's certainly built for it," Phoebe agreed. John's muscles were definitely cover-man stuff, but she found her eyes sliding back to the instructor.

"Hi, Paul." Angie's voice held flirtatious overtones. She stopped beside a compact, bearded redhead who was pulling a warm-up jacket out of an athletic bag. "Haven't seen you here for a while."

"Hi, Angie." Paul seemed inclined to chat, so Phoebe wandered away. She knew her friend used the club partly as a way to meet men. It was better than a singles' bar, she supposed vaguely, but still . . . it seemed like a lot of effort just for the dubious pleasure of masculine company. Anyway, Angie had assured her that as a good Italian girl she wasn't interested in anything else—for the most part.

Of course, Angie's idea of friendship was different from hers: it included dating, going out a lot, having several admirers with whom to flirt. Phoebe sighed. In theory she knew all about how the game was to be played or, at least, how Angie played it. The vivacious young bookkeeper had been one of the first tenants to rent a room in the big old house Phoebe and Danny had owned in Kirkwood—the house that, despite the presence of two small boys and a very large dog, had seemed so empty after Danny's death.

From the beginning the two women had got along well. But they had their differences. For Angie, masculine admiration was essential. She had never stopped prodding her landlady to lose weight, wear push-up bras, find a man friend. Now Phoebe was finally listening to Angie's directives, and all because Tanner Hayden threatened to reenter her life.

She caught a glimpse of herself in the giant mirror that covered one wall and nearly groaned aloud. She'd never had pretensions to glamour. At thirty-two, after widowhood and motherhood, she looked like what she was: a comfortable, undemanding woman, a lover of cookies and pastries, a woman whose most aerobic action heretofore had been riding a bicycle to the drugstore. Her kind wouldn't rate a second glance from a man like Tanner Hayden, television's latest macho hero.

Her hair was simply brown—not glossy black like Angie's, not gleaming auburn like her oldest son's. It was shiny enough, she thought dispassionately, but that was all it had going for it. When it got in her way, she cut it herself in a ragged urchin style that framed her face haphazardly. Her face was all right, too—just all right. Regular brown eyes, regular nose, mouth a little too wide, a little too full.

But it was her body that came in for censure. Newly awakened to a consciousness of bodies by all the perfect ones around her, Phoebe looked helplessly at her own well-padded collection of muscles and tissues. Not exactly skinny to begin with, she'd put on a few extra pounds when she'd been pregnant with Jamie six years ago and added a few more with Brendan. Danny hadn't minded. His death a few months after Brendan's birth had precipitated a few more pounds. Somehow an extra serving of pasta, a fresh batch of cookies, had been ways of trying to fill the empty place he'd left in her life.

Now the evidence of her indulgence was obvious. Her hips were full, her arms and thighs well rounded, her breasts thrust prominently against her faded T-shirt. Compared to the thin, fit bodies parading around the health club, she looked positively Rubenesque.

She had less than three months to take her overblown thirty-two-year-old body and reduce it to reasonably slim twenty-year-old proportions. There were less than three months before Tanner Hayden would arrive for on-location filming. He wanted—or so his letter had told her—to get back in touch, to recapture the rapture of their youthful affair.

Phoebe turned away from the mirror in despair and bumped into the instructor, who stood right behind her. "Sorry," she mumbled. He didn't move. Those piercing blue eyes were fixed on her as if he'd understood every thought in her head.

They stared at each other for a moment before he spoke. "I just wanted to tell you—" he was watching her face intently "—that if you were thinking of climbing into the Jacuzzi, you should wait half an hour or so. Easier on your heart."

My heart, Phoebe thought, feeling confused. It was her outside she'd been concerned about. But of course aerobic exercise was supposed to benefit the heart.

"I'm really not here for the Jacuzzi or my heart," she blurted, voicing her thought. "I just want to drop some pounds."

As soon as the words were out she wanted to call them back. How uncool! If her face hadn't already been as red as a fire truck from the exercise, she would have blushed from her ill-fated tongue, the curse of her existence. With difficulty she controlled the impulse to compound her blunder by excusing it. What did it matter, after all? It was nothing to her if the instructor found something lacking in her body—or vice versa.

At least he didn't laugh. Instead he flicked a cursory glance over her, and she could have sworn that his gaze lingered on her breasts and rounded belly. "A little out of condition," he said, dismissing it.

His eyes held hers, narrowing slightly. She could look away—her gaze shifted nervously over his shoulder. But she had to look back. He was still watching her warmly, intently. "Are you a member of the club?"

She shook her head. "Angie brought me." Her voice came out in an almost incoherent croak. Clearing her throat, she tried again. "Just visiting."

He leaned one shoulder against the wall, his whole body expressing leisurely enjoyment. His skin was very smooth, with fluid muscles evident beneath the surface. There was perceptible grace in even his smallest movements.

"I'm new here, too," he told her. "Ross is letting me use his equipment in return for teaching the class." He smiled, and she noticed again the delightful way a smile affected his eyes. "New in class, new in town. My name's Merlin Brown."

He held out his hand, and she looked at it for a minute before she remembered what to do. "Uh, Phoebe Sullivan," she said, putting her hand in his. Instead of the brisk shake and withdrawal she'd intended, he held her hand motionless, sandwiching it gently between both of his while he examined her face again with that disconcerting blue gaze.

"I don't mean to stare." The husky note in his voice grew more pronounced. Where he held her hand, she felt a strange fuzzy sensation in her nerves.

"So Monk ol' buddy, how'd it go?" The mood was shattered when a craggy-faced blond giant clapped Merlin on the shoulder, then transferred his attention to Phoebe, smiling in a friendly way. "Who's this?"

"Phoebe Sullivan," Phoebe said again. "I'm a friend of Angie's."

"Ah, the beauteous Angie," the giant said, rolling his eyes toward the ceiling.

"Did I hear my name taken in vain?" Angie drifted up, closing the snap fastener of the jeans she'd pulled on over her leotard. "Ross, darling, it was fun not to have you blundering around all over the place today." She flicked a glance at Merlin. "Your replacement did just fine."

Ross linked his arm through hers exuberantly. "I never pretended to be an aerobics instructor. Monk is going to handle that for me for a while."

"Monk?" Phoebe spoke first. "Are you—celibate?"

"Phoebe!" Angie laughed gaily, stepping on Phoebe's foot. Ross, too, emitted a frank gust of laughter.

"It's a fair question," Merlin said, smiling. "I had the misfortune to grow up with clowns who pinned a nickname on everyone. Monk was the one they dished out to me." He forestalled Phoebe's next words. "Because I liked to climb."

Ross shook his head tolerantly. "You didn't just like to climb, buddy. You spent your formative years in trees and atop garages." He turned to Phoebe. "I broke a lot of bones trying to keep up with him." He clapped his childhood friend on the shoulder again, jolting him against the mirror. "Let's go next door for a cup of coffee. You ladies want to join us?"

Phoebe didn't. She felt weak and sweaty, and all she could think of was getting home and hobbling into a hot bath. But Angie wanted to go with the guys, and she'd ridden over in Angie's car.

They walked out of the club and around the corner to Kirkwood Road, the village's main drag. If one followed it far enough north, it became Lindbergh Boulevard and led to the St. Louis airport. But for Kirkwood residents it was simply the center of their downtown. A Saturday-morning bustle filled the street and sidewalks. Phoebe was grateful for the chilly breeze against her hot cheeks.

Mabel's Coffee Shop was a local meeting place, small and crowded. Phoebe tried not to see the doughnuts and coffee cakes prominently displayed at the counter. She stood by the cash register with her modest cup of tea and watched from the corner of her eye as Ross selected a monstrous confection to go with his coffee. Merlin stood beside her, examining a crowded bulletin board that hung by the door.

Angie paid for her coffee just as he reached out to tear off one of the phone numbers that fringed a For Rent sign on the board. "Looking for a place to live?" She sidled up to Monk and treated him to the look she'd told Phoebe she called "man-melter number one." "Phoebe happens to have a vacancy right now."

Monk turned to look at Phoebe with renewed interest as Ross led the way to a booth. "You rent apartments?"

"Rooms," she corrected him, suddenly nervous. The way he looked at her had an extraordinary effect on her. She hadn't felt so strange since the early days of her courtship with Danny. "I—I live in a big old house, and I rent rooms out to boarders. Angie's one."

"It's funky, but comfortable," Angie chimed in. "Of course, you have to like children, dogs and bird-watchers."

Phoebe smiled weakly as everyone at the table looked at her. "Two children. Six and four. One dog, age indeterminate. One bird-watcher, fifty-four and motherly." She thought for a moment. "Very motherly. But not as loud as the boys or the dog."

There was a brief silence while the occupants of the booth digested this information. She didn't look at Monk, who sat beside her, but she could feel questions emanating from him. Before he could ask any of them, Angie rushed into a speech.

"Of course, I don't notice the noise much because I'm at work all day. And Phoebe's mother is really a sweet person, despite the binoculars." She leaned across the booth and gazed soulfully at Monk. "Man-melter number two," Phoebe thought, watching Angie in action with the kind of fascination she would accord a snake charmer. "Why don't you come on by and look at the room?"

Monk smiled at her casually and turned to look at Phoebe. She was somehow pleased to note that "man-melter number two" had had so little effect. "Is there a yard?"

She blinked and answered warily. "Yes." He waited, and at last she elaborated. "A big backyard, but it's kind of...cluttered." She wafted one hand vaguely in the air. "Children, you know. And there's storage in the garage and cellar—the cellar if you have things you want to keep dry. The rent includes food—dinners, breakfasts. You'd have to share a bath with the other roomers."

"I wouldn't mind," Angie cooed. Phoebe felt a moment's exasperation. Monk wasn't the kind to fall for such blatant lures—she didn't know how she knew, but she did. Angie was making a fool of herself.

"Angie, stop the Suzanne Sommers act and give the man a chance to think about it." As usual, the words were out of her mouth before she knew she was going to say them. "Sorry," she mumbled contritely.

The bench quivered with Monk's efforts to repress his laughter. Ross didn't bother to try; he flung back his head and roared. Angie's eyes darkened ominously, but she contented herself with stepping on Phoebe's foot again.

"I think I'd like to look at the room. Would this afternoon be all right?" Monk's voice was smooth, but the undercurrent of amusement was still there. Phoebe despised herself for reacting to it, so her answer was gruffer than she meant it to be.

"Sure." She looked beseechingly at Angie. "Are you ready to go? Mom has a field trip today, and I have to be back before she leaves."

Angie waited until they were driving in her car toward Phoebe's house before she opened fire. "I thought you had overcome your habit of running off at the mouth," she said with the bluntness of friendship.

"I thought so, too," Phoebe answered miserably. "I don't know what came over me."

"Well, I do." Angie glanced sideways at her. "Ross's friend is certainly good-looking."

"You think so?" Phoebe made her voice sound casual and kept her face turned toward the window. "Sort of swarthy for my taste."

"He seemed pretty taken with you."

"Impossible." She gnawed at her lower lip. "How could someone in such good shape be interested in someone like me?" She looked down at her ample lap.

"I don't know," Angie said with more candor than kindness, "but he certainly is. And if you wanted him, all you needed to do was take me aside for a minute. I would have ceased my attack." She gave an angry sniff. "You didn't have to embarrass me in front of them."

Phoebe reached over and patted Angie's hand. "I'm sorry, honey. I wasn't thinking, as usual."

Mollified, Angie swung into the driveway. "Well, he'll be good practice material for you until your friend Tanner blows into town." She sighed in frank envy. "It's all wasted on you, I swear. A man like Tanner Hayden in your past, and you never say one word about it. And now this Monk is interested, and you don't seem enthusiastic at all." Angie shook her head. "No thrill of the chase, that's your problem. And the capture—ah!" She rolled her eyes and climbed out of the car.

Phoebe climbed out, too, looking at her house as a stranger might, as Monk Brown might this afternoon. It was old, as she'd told him, built at the turn of the century when families were large, and cheap heat had made such houses possible. With a partial attic above, it stood two stories tall on its roomy lot. The front steps led up to a wide veranda, a part of it screened in, that extended along three sides of the house. Big windows let in the light—and also drafts during the winter. High ceilings contributed an airy spaciousness—and difficulty in heating.

But with all its faults, she loved the house. She and Danny had bought it just before Brendan's birth. They had planned to fix it up as the money became available and to bring it back to its proud days of glory.

Then Danny had died, and Phoebe was hard put just to make the payments. The house was getting shabbier and shabbier, its paint peeling, its porch sagging, its roof looking moth-eaten. She had done what she could with grout and Spackle, but that wasn't enough to arrest the gentle downward slide of her property. . . .

The front door banged open, and two little boys burst out, their shrill greetings swallowed up in the frantic barking of the huge animal that crowded next to them.

"Mom! Mom! We're making cookies!"

"Mom! I picked up all my toys!"

"Are we going to the park now?"

"Hey, Mom! Rufus threw up in the living room!"

Phoebe knelt and gathered the two wriggly bodies into her arms. She looked at the small-elephant shape that was Rufus, digging up her newly sprouted daffodil bulbs; at the sagging steps of her home; at the tall, spare figure of her mother standing in the doorway. No matter how you sliced it, life was good. She threw back her head and laughed.

"Did I hear cookies!" All thoughts of a hot bath were banished with her sons' hugs. "Lead me to them!"

2

IT WAS LATE AFTERNOON when Monk showed up to look at the vacant room. Phoebe had had her hot bath after fixing a mound of sandwiches and fruit for her kids and the boarders to help themselves to. In keeping with her new vows of weight control, she'd contented herself with cottage cheese and half an apple. But the cookies the boys had made that morning still smelled temptingly good. Piled on a plate beside the sink, they seemed to call to her when she reached for a drink of water. She was guiltily cramming a last bite of one into her mouth when the doorbell pealed.

Monk stood in front of the rickety screen door, his hands in the back pockets of his faded jeans as he surveyed the wide comfortable veranda. Faintly from the backyard came the shouts of the boys working on the dam they were building in an unused corner of the garden.

Phoebe felt an odd rush of quivery excitement as she pushed the screen door open. She'd paid more attention to her appearance than usual after her bath, pulling on pleated gray pants and a long free-floating tunic liberally embroidered with flowers by her mother's clever fingers. She was too honest not to admit to herself that her primping was due to Monk's expected arrival. But she didn't understand why she was going to so much trouble. After all, it was Tanner who was on her mind these days. Nevertheless, at the sight of Monk's lean body on the porch, her heart gave a jolt.

He turned as the door groaned, and she barely had time to notice once again the way his hair erupted into a cowlick at the back of his head before he was smiling at her with a slow, easy friendliness that took her breath away. "I like your house."

It was the last thing she'd expected him to say. Surprise had her gaping for a moment. "Thanks. Most people think it's a little run-down." She stepped out the door and swept a bemused stare over the peeling paint of the front porch.

His shrug was dismissive. "Well, that's no crime. It has heart."

His words were simple, direct. But the message she got from his bright blue eyes was infinitely more complex. A half-forgotten warmth started in her solar plexus, radiating upward through her body—and downward, too. She grabbed for the screen door and held it open. "So do you want to see the room?" Her voice came out sounding breathless.

His lips quirked again, but his face was suitably grave. "That's what I came for." Again he managed to invest the pedestrian words with a wealth of meaning.

She turned toward the stairs, not waiting to see if he followed her. "It's up here. The boarders have the second floor. There's no air-conditioning, but we do have ceiling fans and most of them work." She knew she was babbling as she led the way up the stairs, but she couldn't seem to stop the words from pouring out of her mouth. "You'd have to share a bath. Did I mention that before?"

She walked along the airy upstairs hall and pushed open a door at the back of the house. The big room was high ceilinged and had plaster walls. A trio of wide windows looked out on the budding branches of a maple tree. Afternoon sun laced the walls with shadows from the trees, dappling the furniture and Monk's face. He glanced around at the wide iron bedstead with its pleasing quilt of faded patchwork, at the comfortable outlines of the bowfront bureau, at the worn chintz of the overstuffed chair. The floorboards were gleaming hardwood, and there was a prim square of Brussels carpet in the middle of the room. The tiebacks at the window were splashed with large, cheerful daffodils.

He walked over to the bed and sat on the edge. It shrieked protestingly, but the mattress didn't sag when he lay down. Hands behind his head, he surveyed the room once again before his eyes met hers.

"Will it do?"

"It's perfect." His gaze strayed back to the windows and the blue-and-white quilt of sky beyond them. "Who's being murdered out there?"

Phoebe peered out the window, which overlooked the backyard. In the far corner the reservoir had evidently come far enough along to require filling. Jamie held the garden hose, and Brendan, his face dripping, was howling with rage and distress.

"No murders. Just simple drowning," she said, sighing. Opening the window, she leaned out. "Jamie, don't use the hose to squirt your brother. Keep the water on the ground or turn it off."

Jamie's face lifted to hers, full of self-righteous indignation. "It was an accident," he bellowed. "He got in the way just as I was filling the dam."

The bed behind her creaked as Monk slid off it and came to join her at the window. His eyes widened at the extent of the mudworks the boys had erected in the yard. "Looks like the Suez Canal." He studied the mud-splattered figures of the little boys for a moment as, enmity forgotten, they returned to the work of flooding the ditch they'd scraped out of the garden area. "So do they."

Phoebe shut the window. "It washes off," she said, dismissing the incident, "and I don't let them do it if it's too chilly." Glancing critically around the room, she straightened the embroidered dresser scarf. "If there's anything you want me to change—"

"Nothing," he said, interrupting her, and the warm currents in his voice flowed through her like honey. "I don't want you to change a thing."

She edged toward the door. "Well, then...you want the room?"

"That, too."

Opening the door, Phoebe stumbled into the hall. "I'll show you where the bathroom is." She wondered why she felt so short of oxygen in a world where everyone else could breathe. "We serve breakfast at seven in the morning, dinner at six in the evening. Weekend meals are pretty casual." She took a deep breath and strove for normalcy. "This is the bathroom."

"I see." He stood right beside her. Together they stared at the big old-fashioned bathroom—the tiny black-and-white octagonal tiles that covered the floor and came halfway up the walls, the massive old claw-foot tub and the equally massive pedestal sink.

"Usually there's no trouble about sharing. Everyone seems to have very different schedules."

"No kidding." The voice came from behind them. In the corridor opposite Monk's new room, a door had opened. Peering out of it was a dark sleep-creased face surmounted by a wild Afro. "Like, my schedule says this is sleep time. You wakin' me up, Landlady."

Phoebe smiled. "Sorry, J.S." She pushed Monk forward a little. "This is our new roomer, Monk Brown. And this grumpy person is our resident musical genius, Johann Sebastian Block."

J.S. stretched one black muscular arm toward Monk, who stepped forward for the obligatory soul-brother grip. Phoebe noticed that he performed it with ease.

"Good to meet you, Monk. I'd come out and say howdy, but Ms Landlady here don't allow no naked people in her hall." J.S. sent Phoebe a lazy smile.

"Damned straight I don't. And never mind the jive talk, J.S. I happen to know you're a Juilliard graduate."

J.S. groaned. "Somebody here got a big mouth," he muttered. "Long as we're talkin', did anyone tell Mr. Monk how come his room is vacated?"

Phoebe frowned. "There's no secret about it, certainly," she said coolly. "Miss Nesbit, the former occupant . . . died."

"Yeah, she stiffed it in her sleep a couple of weeks ago." J.S. spoke the words with relish. "She was a great old dame, but she had a bee in her bonnet about spirits. Told me she'd be hanging around here to check everything out after she croaked."

"J.S., have a little respect!" Phoebe turned to Monk apprehensively. "Miss Nesbit was eccentric about spiritualism, but I refuse to believe that she haunts my house. She was far too polite for that."

The door to Monk's new room suddenly blew shut.

They stood in the hall for a moment in silence. Monk regarded his door with an inscrutable expression. With a delighted chuckle J.S. began to move back into his room. "She was a spunky old gal, all right. Nice to have you back, Miss Nesbit."

He shut his own door, and Phoebe and Monk were left to stare at each other in the airy upper hall. Monk broke the silence. "Are the other residents of the rooming house more . . . corporeal?"

Phoebe laughed. "Of course." She tried to infuse her voice with confidence. "That was just a coincidence, you know."

"Naturally."

The dryness of his voice gave her pause. She turned away. "You've met Angie, and that just leaves Edith." Indicating the door down the hall from J.S.'s, she knocked.

After a moment the door opened. A woman stuck her head around the edge of it, rather like J.S. had, Phoebe thought. But it would never occur to anyone that this woman was naked. She looked as if she had never been and would never be naked.

"Edith, I'd like you to meet our new roomer. This is Merlin Brown. Monk, this is Edith Reber. Edith's a librarian."

Edith allowed a bit more of herself to emerge from her room. She was tall, thin and gangly, her forehead carved with a shortsighted frown. The thick-lensed glasses seemed too heavy for the bridge of her nose. Her mousy hair was scraped back into a tight braid that wound around the back of her head. As usual, she carried a book, her finger holding her place in it.

"Glad to meet you," she mumbled. Phoebe felt the mixture of sympathy and exasperation that Edith always produced in her.

Monk stepped closer and took Edith's hand, nearly having to pry it off the doorframe. Looking keenly into her face, he said, "I'm going to enjoy living here. It seems to be populated by interesting people—and other things as well." He shot Phoebe a mischievous look.

Edith withdrew her hand. "Yes, of course." She glanced once at Monk, then nodded to Phoebe and began to close the door. "Nice . . . see you at dinner."

Phoebe took Monk's arm without realizing it, tugging him toward the stairs. When they were halfway down, she felt a tremor of awareness that was like a delayed reaction starting through her hand, and she let go. To distract herself she spoke of Edith. "That poor woman. I don't know what it would take to lure her out of her shell. Or even if it's a good idea."

They reached the downstairs hall, dominated by an old-fashioned crystal chandelier, and she led the way into the living room. Monk followed her, looking around at his new home. "How long has she been here?"

"Almost a year—can you believe it? And I've never gotten more than five words at a time out of her." Phoebe stopped for a moment, looking around. "Oh, yes. This is the living room. You're welcome to use it anytime. Mother and the boys and I have our private quarters across the hall."

The living room was comfortably cluttered. There was a huge old couch slipcovered in a chintz that would have been unbearably gaudy if it hadn't faded into respectability. Two overstuffed chairs confronted a small TV at one side of the long room. Against one wall was a massive oak library table covered with the pieces of a big incomplete jigsaw puzzle. "J.S. likes to do those," Phoebe remarked, catching the direction of Monk's glance.

She led the way through a wide archway that separated the living room from the dining room. They skirted the scarred mahogany dining table, stretched to its utmost capacity by three leaves and surrounded by a motley collection of chairs. "Kitchen in here." The swing door to the kitchen was propped open.

The kitchen was big, with an old-fashioned gas range in one corner and a freezer beside the back door. Counters and cabinets were scarce, but wide shelves covered one whole wall down to waist height. Glass jars of flour and grains, pasta and beans, stacks of china and rows of glasses gleamed in orderly progression. Near the sink was a portable dishwasher.

Phoebe looked around contentedly. "It's a little old-fashioned, but we manage with it."

Monk watched her as she moved around the room. She took chickens out of the refrigerator and prepared them for the oven with capable ease. The spring sunlight poured through west-facing windows and lit golden highlights in her soft brown hair. In spite of the sophisticated pants and shirt she wore, she looked right at home in the anachronistic atmosphere the kitchen managed somehow to project.

He perched on a corner of the pine worktable that took up the center of the room. "How did you come to start a rooming house, anyway? This must be the last one of its kind anywhere in the world."

Phoebe collected the ingredients for piecrust and carried them to the table, where she sat down. "What you're asking for is the story of my life," she warned, keeping her voice light. "I never know where to start when someone asks me why I do what I do."

He moved a bit as she scattered flour over the surface of the table. "Just start at the beginning and go on to the end. I want to hear it all."

"Really?" She looked up, skeptical, but her eyes fell before the intent warmth in his.

"Really. For instance, your sons must have had a father. Where is he?"

"He's dead." Phoebe looked apologetic at the starkness of her words. "He died almost four years ago. We bought the house a few months before Brendan was born. And a few months after he was born, Danny got meningitis. We didn't realize what it was until it was too late." She looked down at the bowl of flour and shortening, concentrating on blending them with her fingertips. "It took me a while to realize that he was gone. I was so calm, so self-contained. Two months after the funeral I went to pieces." When she looked up, she found it almost painful to meet his compassionate gaze.

"You were left with a lot of responsibilities."

"You said it." She pushed the bowl away and began absently rubbing her fingers together to clean off the dough. "I was nursing Brendan, and my milk dried up overnight. He wasn't too happy about that. We were living on the insurance money, and I knew it wouldn't last forever. Then my mother came to stay. She helped me pull myself together." One blob of the dough wouldn't come off, and she scraped at it with a fingernail. "Angie had worked in Danny's office, and when she was forced out of her apartment it seemed natural to rent her one of our unused bedrooms. The boarding-house aspect started because no one could keep track of their food. I thought it would be simpler to provide meals than to have so many people swarming around in the kitchen."

Monk looked around. Despite its cozy charm, the kitchen had a rickety look. Everything seemed patched together. "Do you make enough to live?"

She laughed ruefully. "Hardly. I make enough to keep the house going, after a fashion. This summer I'll be able to have the roof fixed and the foundation repaired. Next summer I hope to be able to paint the whole blooming place." She pulled back the bowl and added water, gathering the piecrust and flattening it onto the table with her usual exuberance.

"So what do you do for food?"

He liked the way she grinned at him, undaunted by her obvious financial problems. "I did some public relations and copywriting before Jamie was born, so I kind of enlarged on that. Now I've built up a clientele of local businesses that I write advertising copy for. If their budget is tight I even do pasteup and layout. Sort of a low-cost, one-woman advertising agency."

"And that pays well?"

"Not exactly." She sighed. "The pay is pretty modest, to tell you the truth. But I don't really have what it takes for a full-time, office-type job. Maybe next year when both the boys are in school I'll concentrate on entering the real business world. Right now we're getting by, and that's always been enough for us."

He felt an unexpected ache of tenderness and protectiveness. He admired her gallantry, even as he wished for the power to make her life easier.

Rolling pin in hand, Phoebe flattened the piecrust. But her mind was on the man in her kitchen, not on her work. She didn't usually tell the story of her life to every stranger she met, although to her chagrin she knew that it took very little encouragement from friends for her to unload her problems. *You're a big blabbermouth,* she told herself. And there was something about this man that invited confidence.

But actually she had very little information about him. He was a lifelong friend of Ross Belden, and she knew Ross vaguely as a local businessman. But for all she knew, his friend could be a mass murderer just released from jail. It had been foolish to agree to rent him a room simply because he seemed so comfortable and familiar, as if she'd known him forever.

"So how about you?" she said bluntly, with her famed propensity for speaking her thoughts. "What's the story of your life?"

Monk smiled easily and handed her the pie plate. "Not too interesting, I'm afraid. I was born and raised in the suburbs—Clayton, just down the road. Spent my childhood falling out of trees, as Ross told you. Entered the family business. Went to San Francisco to handle the branch operations and discovered my true vocation."

"Which is?"

"Clowning around," he answered promptly.

Phoebe nearly tore the piecrust. She allowed herself one skeptical glance at him before she concentrated on getting the crust into the plate in one piece. Taking a bowl of apples off the counter behind her, she began to peel and slice them expertly into the crust. "What do you really do?"

"A little bit of everything, like all jesters do." He looked around the kitchen then took three apples from the bowl in front of her. "Let me show you."

Phoebe held her paring knife suspended as Monk began to juggle the apples, clumsily at first, as if he was about to drop each one.

"You don't look too good at it," she gasped. One apple narrowly missed the shelf holding wineglasses.

"It's harder than it looks," he complained. "All the same, I think I just . . . might . . . be able to manage . . . one more." Still juggling the three original apples, he reached for another one without looking. And somehow, instead of a fourth apple, he came up with Phoebe's paring knife.

"Watch out!" Her voice came out in a high squeak. "I just had that sharpened!"

"Goodness me," Monk said mildly. His juggling still appeared clumsy, as if disaster was only a half second away, but suddenly Phoebe realized that it took quite a bit of skill to look so clumsy and not have an accident. The three apples and the paring knife whizzed through the air, and she watched, her heart in her mouth, as Monk dropped the paring knife and came up with another apple.

"Man, these things are making me hungry." He smacked his lips, making the four apples revolve around his head. Somehow he managed to keep three of them in the air while he took a quick bite of the fourth one. "That was good. I'll just finish it off." Still juggling the apples, he kept biting away at the one he'd started on until it was merely a core. "Just what the doctor ordered," he said at last, dropping the uneaten apples one at a time into the bowl and flipping the core into the trash.

Phoebe let her breath out. "Some performance."

Monk shrugged. "Pretty standard," he said, then grinned at her, a sudden flash of good humor that left her breathless. "Actually, it got a bit tricky for a minute there. I'm usually juggling three, not four apples, when I eat one."

Phoebe took up her paring knife and began working on the apples he'd dropped back into her bowl, her mind whirling. "So you really are a performer. But then why are you teaching aerobic dancing?"

"I told you—I need a gym to work out in, so I don't get out of shape. For teaching the class I get the run of the gym. Ross is even going to let me put up the slack rope in a corner."

Phoebe summoned up a memory of the big three-ring circus she'd taken the boys to a couple of years ago. "You do tightrope stuff, too?" With a lavish hand she scattered cinnamon and sugar over the apples, dotted them with butter and began rolling out a top crust.

"Slack rope," he corrected her. "I don't have the equipment or the crew it takes for high-wire stuff. Slack rope is done close to the ground and is less demanding physically."

"And that's part of your act?"

He moved uneasily. "It's a circus technique, certainly. What I do is more rooted in mime and the commedia del l'arte tradition. You know, those ancient Italian performance techniques that Shakespeare used so often in his comedies. It's really what got me started." His clever fingers twirled the stem out of an apple while he talked. "I did a lot of acting in college, and for that I had to learn tumbling, fencing, that sort of thing. In San Francisco I saw troupes that put together acrobatics, dance, mime and improv to create street entertainment. Presto! I was hooked."

"To the point of quitting your family's business?" Phoebe didn't mean to sound nosy, but after all, if he was going to be living in her house, she should know as much as possible about him. That was a good excuse, anyway. "I mean, it seems kind of drastic. . . ."

"Call it an early midlife crisis." Monk shrugged, looking a little uncomfortable. "I do have some regret about quitting," he admitted after a moment. "But the job was so demanding! There was never a moment for anything I wanted to do that would. . . refresh my spirit. Do you understand?"

She met his eyes for a moment and was captured by the urgency and forthrightness in that vivid gaze. She forced herself to drop her eyes and found herself mentally stripping off his shirt to see again the muscular economy that had stirred her that morning. Feverishly she cut steam vents in her pastry and fitted the top crust over the apples. But the memory of his smooth, strong torso stayed with her, accompanied by an unfamiliar emotion—one she hadn't felt in years. Desire.

Her hands automatically crimped the pastry, but her mind wasn't on the small task she performed. Glancing at Monk from the corner of her eye, she saw that his own gaze was bent on her swift-moving fingers. Then he raised his head, and their eyes met.

With a jolt that was almost audible, her heart stopped. Then it revved up, pounding in her chest until she felt faint. His eyes were so crystalline clear, so compelling she was unable to look away. She knew he would be able to see her physical attraction to him, but she didn't know how to conceal what she felt. The intensity of the emotion was bewildering.

His eyes narrowed slightly, and he lifted her motionless hands from the piecrust. Leaning across the table, he pulled gently until she inclined toward him. She moved slowly, sweetly, feeling as if each motion was drowned in a honeyed syrup. When he brought his mouth to hers with a gentle touch, the honey seemed to spread inside her. She let her mouth cling to his, amazed and delighted at the sweetness she found there.

Then his tongue flicked out, and somehow she was pulled out of her chair, was pressed against him while something wild and dark surged through her and submerged the honey. Her body awoke to long-dormant needs. Breasts, pelvis, mouth, all began to hunger restlessly for something she hadn't even realized she lacked. It was too much, too overpowering. Her eyelids lifted regretfully, and she pushed against his shoulders.

When he stepped away, her body protested against the abrupt withdrawal of pleasure. There was some satisfaction in noting that his chest heaved and that his hand as he passed it over his brow was unsteady. When he spoke, however, his voice was just the same. "I didn't mean to get out of line."

She turned back to the piecrust, but knew better than to attempt to finish it with her shaky hands. "I...didn't, either." She wished vainly for the sophistication to carry the situation off with a light touch. "It . . . I don't know why. . ." As usual, her befuddled brain blurted out its every thought. "After all, there's Tanner—"

The warmth in his eyes vanished. "Who's Tanner? Your boyfriend?"

Phoebe shook her head, trying to subdue her confusion. "I shouldn't have said that." She looked at Monk and melted, unable to resist the impulse to pour out everything to this man who watched her warily but with yearning in the depths of his eyes. For some inexplicable reason he was attracted to her—Phoebe, the perennially overweight, the blunt of tongue and soft of body. So while she finished the pie, she told him about Tanner.

She had been a freshman in college, her first time away from home, wide-eyed and eager for life. He was older—out of the Army—handsome and suave, his conventional looks incongruous with his slightly radical views. He had been her first lover.

"He had an off-campus apartment," Phoebe recalled, bending over to put the pie in the oven. She hoped the heat of the stove would seem to account for the flush she felt on her cheeks. "We used to go there in the afternoons. It seemed so beautiful, so free." She laughed. "There was a lot of rebellion and revolution going on then. It was a great time to be young and away from home. I enjoyed myself immensely."

"What happened?" Monk kept his eyes on her face.

Phoebe shrugged. "One afternoon I came by to see why he hadn't kept our date in the student union. He was in bed—with another woman. He pointed out to me that true revolutionaries, true exponents of free love, didn't believe fidelity was necessary. Intellectually I could buy it. Emotionally I couldn't. I stopped seeing him. A few months later I met Danny, and everything seemed to fall into place. We were married right after graduation. Danny got a job with the city utilities department, and I worked part-time doing public relations for a radio station. We were so happy."

She looked down at her hands, blinking away the ready tears. Even four years later, Danny's death had the power to move her. She had given up wondering why they hadn't been allowed more time together. She had even given up railing against the fates for visiting death on anyone as vibrant and alive as Danny Sullivan. But she still hadn't given up tears.

Monk put his hand on hers, and this time the warm current flowing between them was comforting, not sexual. He cleared his throat. "You must have really loved the guy."

"I'll always love Danny." She raised her face and smiled at him. "But I'm not—I don't *idolize* his memory or anything. Only Danny's life stopped, not mine."

He squeezed her hand and moved away, leaning against the sink, his arms folded over his chest. The sensual awareness was back in his eyes as he asked, "So what's the problem?"

She gulped. "Well, it's Tanner—like I told you."

His brows drew together. "He cheated on you, and you dropped him. That's all you told me."

She looked around the kitchen. There must be something more she could do for dinner that would keep her hands occupied. She took potatoes from the root cabinet and went over to the sink to wash them. It was something to do, but it brought her uncomfortably close to that taut, muscular body.

"I didn't tell you about the letter? Well, Tanner wrote me a letter a couple of weeks ago. I used to hear from him sporadically after I got married—the kind of letters you suspect are meant to make you sorry you threw over a good thing." She glanced at Monk. "They never made me feel like that. But he'd just then heard of Danny's death and was giving his condolences and all. And then he said his TV show was doing some location shots in St. Louis this summer, and he looked forward to getting together with me again—'try to undo the absent years,' I think was how he put it."

Monk snorted. Phoebe allowed herself a smile.

"So he's Tanner Hayden, the TV playboy-detective."

"Yes, didn't I mention that?" She scrubbed pensively at a potato. "I don't watch his show, although I did turn it on after getting his letter." She sighed. "So much violence! And all those women writhing over him. Not much of the revolutionary left, I'm afraid."

"Is that why you wanted to drop a few pounds? So you could compete with those TV bimbos?"

Phoebe flinched. He kept his voice level, but the words seemed to scorch her.

"Actually, I've been trying to lose weight for a few months now." She glanced at the plate of cookies wistfully. "Just not having much luck. And after Angie found out about Tanner, she thought—"

Monk moved fast, surprising her. He gripped her arms, and a potato hit the sink with a dull clunk. "Listen, Phoebe. You are a very sweet and desirable woman. Your body is only one part of you, and not the most important part. Remember that."

He let her go, and blinking, she stared up at him. Then a slow smile spread across her face. "Thanks," she said huskily. "I needed that." A hint of doubt crept into her voice. "But I need to lose weight, too. It's not healthy to carry thirty extra pounds around all the time. And . . ." She turned back to the potatoes, ashamed of the pettiness of her thought.

Monk wouldn't let her retreat. "And?"

She finished the last potato before speaking. "Well, I wasn't this fat when I first knew Tanner. In fact, he's never seen me looking like this. I'd just feel . . . humiliated somehow for him to see me so overweight." She turned and looked resolutely at Monk. "I know that's a stupid attitude. But I can't help it."

Monk sighed. He was beginning to feel something stirring around inside him, something strong that he'd never felt for any woman before. The corporate types who'd attracted his attention had been more interested in climbing the ladder to success than in dating a man whose hobbies were unicycle riding and knife throwing. The women friends he had were mostly already in long-term relationships.

But something seemed to be telling him that in Phoebe he'd found the perfect woman for him. Her sweetness, her humor—he could fall in love with her. And she'd be busy trying to look good for some other guy. With a sense of shock he realized that he wanted her to stay the way she was so she'd be camouflaged and less likely to attract competition.

He straightened. "I won't be selfish," he muttered, to Phoebe's obvious bewilderment. Then he smiled down into her worried brown eyes. "Okay. You want to lose weight. I don't care about that, but I can understand wanting to get into shape. I'll help you."

Now there was a frown between her straight brows. "You'll help me look good for another man?"

Was that a spark of chagrin he saw? His smile widened. "Not at all. I'll help you get in shape for *you*. We'll worry about this Tanner clown when he shows up." *If he shows up,* Monk added mentally. Maybe the great TV star would break a leg falling out of his starlet-strewn bed.

In the meantime, he would help Phoebe. And by helping her he'd get to spend time with her. In fact . . . "You know," he said conversationally, helping her place the potatoes on a roasting tray, "you were great to kiss, but I felt you were a bit out of practice. I think you need to get into shape in that department, too."

He met her suspicious gaze limpidly, and after a moment Phoebe smiled. "You may be right," she murmured.

He was reaching out to pull her closer when the back door slammed, and two small bodies hurled themselves into the kitchen.

"Mom! Is dinner ready? What time do we eat?"

"Hey, Jamie trampled all over the Panama Canal!"

"Well, you squished mud on my feet!"

"Hey, who's that guy?"

Two pairs of angelic blue eyes turned up toward Monk. Two pairs of grimy legs deposited bits of the Panama Canal on the clean, faded linoleum of the floor.

Resigning himself to the inevitable, Monk postponed all thoughts of furthering Phoebe's sensual education. He squatted down until his face was even with theirs. "Hello, boys. I'm Monk. Which one of you is which?"

3

DINNER THAT EVENING was the usual cheerful pandemonium. Monk was on hand, having moved his things with Ross's help just before dinner. He didn't have much to take up to his room, although he'd unloaded several mysterious bundles and bags from his old VW bus in the garage.

Refusing Angie's invitation to dinner, Ross had gone off. Shortly after Brendan had beaten the brass dinner gong, Monk took his place in the dining room.

The food was set out on an old-fashioned buffet behind the table. Phoebe watched as Monk went around with J.S., who could put away an amazing amount of food for someone with such a compact body. Angie followed them, automatically blinking her long lashes at Monk as he politely offered her the bread basket. As usual, Edith crept into the room, put a chicken wing and a little salad on her plate and sat down as far away from everyone else as she could.

Phoebe sat at the head of the table with Brendan at her right, so that she could help him with any problems he might have. Her mother was at her left, with Jamie next in line. Angie sat beyond Brendan, chatting vivaciously with J.S. while casting alluring glances at

Monk, who was across from them. At the foot of the table, her isolation almost tangible, was Edith, who kept her eyes on her plate as she picked at her food.

Angie began interrogating Monk for the edification of the whole table. Although Phoebe knew Angie's flirtatious ways were second nature, she nevertheless had to fight to suppress her increasing impatience.

"So where do you do this performing stuff, Monk?" Angie's voice was sweet, her expression one of breathless anticipation.

Monk finished chewing a bite of chicken. "Nowhere, right now. I'm living off my savings while I try to start my own troupe."

"Your own troupe—how thrilling!" Angie paused for thought. "But . . . will you work at kids' birthdays, or what? Where *do* clowns work?"

Monk looked amused. "Wherever they're needed." Phoebe suppressed an involuntary sputter of laughter, and he exchanged a good-natured glance with her before turning back to Angie. "In California I toured with a group of acrobats and mimes who did benefit performances and fund-raisers. A nonprofit group would often sponsor them for a cut of their take. It was a living, although not a lavish one."

"Goodness, no." Angie stared at him in consternation. "I don't see how anyone could survive doing that." She attacked her baked potato, a petulant frown pushing out her lips.

"It's a pretty good idea, actually," Phoebe said. "Lots of organizations have the dullest fund-raisers possible—hospitals, schools—"

"The Audubon Society," her mother put in.

"Well . . ." Phoebe looked doubtful.

"I don't know if what I do would be appropriate for the Audubon Society," Monk said, "but Phoebe's right about the other groups. The Pickle Family Circus goes up and down the west coast from Portland to San Diego every summer and gets a good crowd at most of their performances. Child-care organizations especially like to sponsor them."

"The Pickle Family Circus." Phoebe smiled. "Is that the group you toured with?"

Monk nodded. "They offered me a permanent job, but I wanted to spread the word through the Midwest. I envision a circuit from Kansas City to Chicago, hitting some smaller places in between."

"But Monk—" Angie offered him her wide-eyed ingenue look "—you said yourself that's only for the summer. Could you make enough at that to keep going in the winter?"

Monk shrugged. "Don't know yet." He turned back to his dinner, and the conversation moved to J.S.'s latest gig, playing with a jazz band at a night spot in Laclede's Landing.

Phoebe barely heard Angie's promise to bring her date there that evening. She was occupied with thoughts of Monk. But the facts she'd gathered about him took second place to the intangibles. The feel of him when she'd been in his arms, his lips against hers, his hands stroking her back, cupping her breast. . . . A hot flush rose in her cheeks, and she raised her eyes from her untouched plate to dart a furtive look at him.

He was watching her, his face grave, only the hint of a smile playing around those well-shaped lips. She stared at his mouth for a moment then met his eyes. Was he feeling what she felt? This electric current that seemed to sizzle and snap almost audibly when they made contact?

Though it took an effort of will to look away, she forced herself to do so. It had been too long since a man had shaken her equilibrium. She had no wish to be submerged by the sensations this one could provoke so easily. Control was essential.

But by the time the table was cleared after dessert, she wondered wildly if control was possible. Helpfully Monk stacked plates, balanced huge piles of crockery and carted them into the kitchen, managing each time he passed her to touch her. Each touch rekindled the emotions that had swept over her with such devastating impact that afternoon. She seemed to read a message in his eyes, one that promised more than a touch if he got the opportunity.

Before she could pull herself together to deal with the problem, Monk was pushing her gently out of the kitchen. "Scram," he said with his irresistible smile. He had somehow managed to finagle Edith into carrying some dishes from the dining room, and now he stopped her attempt at headlong flight. "My minions and I will make these dirty dishes vanish. You go relax somewhere."

Phoebe looked at her little boys and Edith. Reluctance was written on their faces. "Your minions don't look too eager for their treat."

"They'll love it." He picked up some cups and began to juggle them while moving toward the dishwasher. The little boys' mouths fell open.

"Hey! Can I do that?" Brendan crowded close, and Monk dropped a cup, barely managing to save it before it could hit the edge of the dishwasher.

"Soon," Monk promised. Edith meanwhile stood transfixed, as if wondering when the loony-bin men would come. Monk glanced at Phoebe and made shooing motions with his hands. "Your dishes are really very safe," he told her. "Now get out of here."

Reluctantly she went, feeling at loose ends without the usual task of straightening the kitchen. She prowled restlessly around the living room, centering the antimacassars perfectly on each round overstuffed chair and sofa back, piling newspapers and magazines in neat pyramids.

"You're making me nervous," her mother said, not looking up from the field guide she pored over.

"Sorry." Phoebe went to look over Elizabeth's shoulder at a page of long-legged birds. "What are you working on?"

"June Morganthal said she spotted a yellow rail at the Busch sanctuary this afternoon." Elizabeth looked up for a moment, her eyes abstracted. "I think it was just a bittern, myself."

Phoebe sprawled in an overstuffed chair and stared blankly at the ceiling. Gradually, instead of the ceiling she saw Monk's face, his lips quirked in a friendly grin, eyes gleaming with sensual intent. He had threatened to give her lessons in kissing—maybe more than kissing. She frowned. If he was attracted to her, how could he stand to tune her up for Tanner, so to speak, and then step aside? And if he wasn't attracted to her, he was doing a damned fine job of acting like he was. . . .

It took a moment before she realized someone was trying to talk to her. "Huh?"

"I said, what you lookin' at up there?" J.S. stood beside her, squinting at the ceiling. "Got a leak in the plaster?"

"Dunno," Phoebe mumbled, her face flaming. She forced herself to bring her emotions under control then ran her eyes over J.S. "Some outfit. Are you going to be in the spotlight tonight?"

"I will be when the other cats see this." He smoothed the sleeve of his white-sequined dinner jacket lovingly. "You gonna come downtown tonight? I'll play something special for you."

Phoebe smiled and shook her head. "Not tonight, J.S. That aerobic dance class really took it out of me." *In more ways than one,* she added silently.

The kitchen door swung open, emitting a gust of childish laughter. Then Edith came out. Phoebe stared at her, amazed. She was smiling—not broadly but definitely—and there was a faint pink flush on her cheeks.

She saw Phoebe and J.S. gaping at her, and some of her defensiveness came back. "The . . . the children are certainly enjoying themselves," she said in a half whisper.

"Sounds like it." Phoebe tried to disguise her amazement at hearing Edith volunteer such a wealth of information. "What's happening in there?"

"Merlin—Monk is teaching them to juggle." Edith sidled nervously past J.S., taking in the flash and glitter of the sequins he wore.

Phoebe groaned, and Edith paused in the door. "With sponges," she assured them earnestly and vanished up the stairs.

J.S. swept a red satin cape around his shoulders. "That woman is bewitched," he said sternly. "He's named Merlin, ain't he? You watch yourself, Landlady." He stalked out the front door.

"Two whole sentences!"

Phoebe spoke to herself, but her mother answered. "That's two sentences more than she's spoken in a year." Elizabeth regarded Phoebe with an unreadable expression for a moment. Then a slow smile crept across her face. "Your new boarder is very... interesting." She closed the field guide and got to her feet. "Think I'll go run the boys' bath. Send them along when they're finished in the kitchen, and I'll get them ready for bed."

Alone in the living room, Phoebe chewed her lower lip and watched the kitchen door nervously. Angie clattered down the stairs and out the door, calling her goodbye to Phoebe with the same breath she used to greet her date. Faintly from the other side of the hall came the sound of running water.

"Watch this, watch this!" The kitchen door burst open, and Jamie raced out, clutching a fistful of cut-up kitchen sponges. He stood in front of her, his face earnest in concentration, and tossed them into the air one at a time. For a moment the three sponges circled obediently through the air. His face split into a triumphant grin. "I can juggle!"

Brendan came out of the kitchen more carefully, his sponges carried like precious treasures. "See!" He threw all three of them into the air at once and laughed as they bounced onto his upturned face.

"Wonderful," Phoebe enthused. "All you guys need is practice to be first-rate."

"I'm going to practice," Jamie vowed. "I'm going to practice every day until I'm as good as Monk. I'm going to be in his troupe and juggle balls and bowling pins and everything!"

Phoebe gathered the warm little bodies to her and hugged them. "I bet you will." They smelled of dish-washing soap and that musky indefinable odor that intense activity produces in small boys. "Grandma's running your bathwater." They groaned in protest, and Phoebe hugged them again. "Bet she'd want to see how you can juggle. Think you can do it in the tub?"

Jamie wiggled free and raced into the hall. "Grandma, Grandma!" He opened the door into the bathroom under the stairs and disappeared, closely followed by his brother. Their voices faded and merged into the sound of the bathwater.

Looking up, Phoebe saw Monk standing in the kitchen doorway.

He leaned against the doorframe, and the fluid lines of his body made a pleasing image. The suspicion of a cowlick at the back of his head was more pronounced. With a dishtowel he was drying his long, clever fingers. Phoebe felt an immediate weakening in her bones at the sight of him.

She couldn't tear her eyes away from his as he walked across the floor toward her and tossed the towel onto the dining room table. "My...mother's giving the boys their bath." Her voice came out an unfamiliar croak.

"Good." He pulled her out of her chair and had her sitting beside him on the couch before she realized it. "That gives us some time to get on with our project."

"Listen, Monk," she said edgily. "I'm not sure what you think—Monk!" His arms had come around her, and now his lips nibbled playfully on her earlobe. "I . . . what project? Why are you—"

"You know what project," he breathed directly into her ear. She closed her eyes helplessly at the shiver of pleasure that went through her. "I'm going to help you loosen up. Warm up, so to speak."

"No kidding." His tongue moved briefly inside her ear, and she squirmed. "You're doing this for another man?"

He grew still for a moment. Then his palms cradled her face and turned her to look at him. "Phoebe." His voice was deeper than usual. "If I'm rushing you into something, I'm sorry. Because I don't want to stop."

Leaning toward her, he kissed her slowly, his mouth both hard and tender on hers, the heat in him catching her by surprise. And yet it wasn't surprise. It was something she'd always known, always needed. She closed her eyes and kissed him back with abandon, feeling the hot flood of desire wash down her body. His teeth nipped at her lower lip then his tongue rubbed wetly along it until she moaned. Her body was flame and light, pulsating with him, craving to have him against her.

She gasped and shuddered and succeeded in pushing him away. "Monk. We can't—"

He leaned his forehead against hers, his breath coming in quick gulps. "I know," he murmured raggedly. "Too much, too soon. Sorry."

"It feels wonderful," Phoebe admitted, her voice small, "but—"

"Don't worry." He gathered her close again, but this time without the overwhelming sensuality. "We'll have to practice some nice, chaste kisses. Like this." Tilting her face up, he pressed a sweet salute on her mouth, breaking it off before it could escalate.

Phoebe sat there, stunned by her reactions, by the galloping need that still thundered in her veins. She didn't want him to kiss her so sweetly, she discovered. She wanted more of that flaming, engulfing passion. That was heady stuff.

"What's the point of any of this?" She shook her head to clear it. "When Tanner gets here, I am going to meet him." She shot a sideways glance at Monk. "Maybe spend a lot of time with him."

He couldn't suppress a scowl. "And maybe not." He reached for her, but she eluded him, springing to her feet.

"The boys may be in any minute." She crossed to the library table, fidgeting absently with a jigsaw puzzle piece. "It'll be time for a chapter of *Peter Pan*."

He stayed on the couch, arms spread along the back, watching her with lively interest. "Wouldn't want them to find you all steamed up with a man," he said equably. She sent him a startled glance and he grinned. "I walked in on my brother Lance one time. He had a reputation as a pretty smooth guy, and it was easy to see why." His grin turned reminiscent. "It was five minutes before he realized I was there—gave me time to absorb a lot of his technique."

"You could have tactfully left," Phoebe murmured. Somehow the mention of his brother triggered an association.

"And miss out on how to perform the famous 'Brown maneuver,' where the partner is clinched, pinned and deprived of oxygen? Let me demonstrate...." He jumped off the couch, but she backed away.

"I think you already did.... Your brother's name is Lance?"

He nodded. "Lancelot Malory Brown. I'm Merlin Malory Brown, and my sister is Elaine Malory Brown. Give you one guess who my mother is."

"Guinevere Malory Brown." Phoebe smiled. "I remember seeing mention of your family in the society pages now and then. Don't they have some big business locally?"

Monk sank back down on the couch and crossed his ankles in front of him. "Ball bearings. One of the largest manufacturers in the country, in fact. Actually—what with diversification and all—the corporation owns a little bit of everything now."

She searched his face to interpret the emotions behind his even words, but could read nothing. "You used to work for them?"

He shifted restlessly. "I wheeled and dealed for a few years after college. But my heart has always been elsewhere." His smile was less genial than usual. "It got to the point where my job was pushing me real hard in one direction. Just one direction—no other interests allowed. Eventually I couldn't take it, so I quit. My mother hasn't yet forgiven me for that."

"Is that why you're not staying with your family?"

Monk got to his feet and prowled around the room. "Just my parents are in the ancestral mansion, if that's what you mean. My brother and sister are both married, with homes of their own. I haven't lived at home since I left for college, so there's no reason why I'd want to now." He stopped in front of her and gazed hungrily down at her. "Listen, all this is past history. I'm no longer Merlin Malory Brown, vice president of financial services for Brown Bearings. I'm a performer. And that's what I really want to be."

"All right already," Phoebe said mildly. "I didn't mean to imply that you have a hang-up about your family or anything."

"I *don't* have a—" Monk bit off his words and took a deep breath. "Just wait until my mother shows up here—which she will—before you get that superior look on your face," he advised pleasantly. "Then maybe you'll understand why I tend to talk about my family through clenched teeth."

Phoebe laughed and turned to the bookcase beside the door. "Sounds intimidating. Why don't you meet her somewhere else and spare me?" She pulled the copy of *Peter Pan* out of the bookcase just as the boys barreled across the hall.

Monk watched the children settle themselves on each side of their mother and listen round eyed while she read with unself-conscious enthusiasm. He had never run across a woman like this before, with her open candid nature and her zest for living. It was a little frightening what she was able to do to him without apparent effort.

"But why did Peter Pan cut off Captain Hook's arm?" The younger one was Brendan, he remembered. Brown hair and brown eyes, like his mother. The eyes were worried now. "Didn't that hurt him?"

"His sword must have really been sharp," the older boy said before Phoebe could answer. That was Jamie—curly hair with a reddish glint and very mischievous blue eyes. "Hey, what was his name before Peter Pan cut off his hand? He didn't have a hook then, did he? So he couldn't have been named Hook, could he? Huh, Mom?"

Phoebe laughed and looked up, and Monk caught her eye. Tearing his own gaze away before it could be noticed by the sharp-eyed children, he got to his feet.

"It's been a long day," he mumbled, "and I wouldn't be able to help you with those questions. See you tomorrow."

He left the living room reluctantly, yawning as he climbed the steps to his room. There was a lot to do the next day. It would be Sunday, so there would be no early-bird aerobics class at the gym. But he'd still have his own workout to do. And he had to find a good place in the garage or the basement for his gear and maybe set up a practice ring in the backyard.

The light was already on in his room, and he wondered if Phoebe had switched it on for him earlier. The room seemed cozy and comfortable, homelike. He puttered around for a while, arranging some of his equipment and costumes in the old-fashioned walk-in closet.

By the time he climbed into the bed he was ready for sleep. He drifted off without realizing that the window curtains stirred gently in the dusky room, although the windows were shut tightly against the chill night air.

4

PHOEBE YAWNED AND WINCED. Muscles she'd never known about had made their presence felt the moment her alarm had rung at six that morning. Now she stood over the oatmeal pot and cautiously stretched. The sorest spots were concentrated in her calves and ribs. She stirred the oatmeal and did a couple of halfhearted knee bends.

The back door opened suddenly, catching her in the middle of a squat, and Monk bounded in, exuding vitality and cheerfulness. Dark patches on the chest of his old gray sweatshirt testified to what he'd been doing. She straightened and glared balefully at him.

"Good morning!" He opened the oven and sniffed deeply. "Fresh-baked muffins! Oatmeal! Man, did I luck out when I came to live here."

Phoebe couldn't help responding to the charm of his smile. That one lock of hair at the back of his head that refused to lie down made him endearing. Her irritation with him began to seep away. She grabbed it back.

"Yes, but what did the rest of us get out of it?" She rubbed the sore muscles along her side. "For instance, I feel permanently crippled by what you put me through yesterday morning."

He slipped a consoling arm around her waist, and his hand, absently massaging the sore spot, felt good, too good. He smelled of fresh spring air and some other, earthier scent that was his alone. She wanted to lean against him, tilt her head back, invite his lips to visit hers.

Instead she moved away, fighting for control. After a couple of sleepless hours last night, she'd made up her mind to keep Monk at a distance. But it was difficult to put space between them. The man-to-woman warmth he offered was so sweet after years of loneliness.

Monk accepted her retreat with a barely perceptible tightening of his expressive mouth. "I've been thinking about what you told me yesterday." His words seemed to drop into sudden silence.

"Which was?" Phoebe glanced at him warily. Those sleepless hours had given her ample time to regret having blabbed so much. Good old Phoebe "the Mouth," guaranteed to blurt out everything, especially if it was personal. She had told Monk a lot more than he needed to know about the life of Phoebe Sullivan.

"You know, about your hotshot TV-star friend dropping in on you." Monk's beguiling smile wasn't reflected in his eyes. "Since I like your boardinghouse and your dinners and your breakfasts so well, I want to help."

Phoebe picked up a pot holder and bent to take the muffins from the oven. It was foolish to feel let down. She had believed that Monk was attracted to her—thirty extra pounds and all. "I remember your help," she muttered. "I don't think I can take much more of it." Uh-oh, now she was running off at the mouth again. She pressed her lips together and tried to keep her face a blank.

Monk saw the hurt in her eyes and longed to soothe it. She was so vulnerable, standing in the early light by the big old stove. He still wasn't sure what he felt, but it was something strong, something unfamiliar. He wanted to comfort her with the strictest chastity then unwrap the quilted kimono she wore and lose himself in the soft satin of her body. . . .

Eventually he realized that he was staring hungrily at her and he blinked. At least she had lost that look of hurt. Whatever she'd seen on his face must have reassured her about his motives.

"I told you I'd help you get into shape, and I meant it," he said simply. "If you want to lose weight, I know how to sweat it off you."

She gave him a skeptical look. "I'll bet."

He hooted with laughter. "You're priceless, Phoebe." He couldn't resist drawing her into his arms, and this time she didn't pull away. The full curve of her breasts touched his chest. All the laughter in her eyes gradually died, replaced with a drowsy intentness that made him shake with longing. He shut his eyes, overwhelmed by the desire to take her to bed, to explore the lazy passion that he knew would flare out of control when he kissed her.

He knew he should draw away, but he had to have just one kiss. "Phoebe—" The word sounded strangled. "About that kissing practice we planned . . ."

Phoebe could hardly bear to look at the crystalline brightness of his eyes. She craved the touch of his lips. "Do you think...I need it?" Taking her question for an answer, he folded his arms more closely around her and touched his mouth to hers.

Instant heat exploded through her. Her lips trembled under his, parting involuntarily. She was pressed against him, against every bulge and muscle emphasized by the soft fabric of his gym clothes. Her hands clutched his shoulders; his were clamping her fiercely to him, while their mouths seemed the center of a flame that branched downward through each body. His desire was evident, its pressure against her strange and yet familiar. She began to drown in the need to be closer.

At last Monk tore his mouth away, gasping. He dropped his cheek against her forehead, loosening his hold as he fought for breath. Phoebe stood limply in the circle of his arms, her mind refusing to take over from her erogenous zones.

Monk took a deep breath. "I'm going to go out and come in all over again." He left her reluctantly and disappeared behind the door. She watched, bemused, as it opened again and he popped through.

"Good morning, Phoebe, m'dear! You have time for one muffin before your workout."

"What workout?" She narrowed her eyes as he pried a muffin out of the tin and juggled it because it was still hot. "It's Sunday. No one works out today."

"You do," Monk said simply. "You will work out every day. We'll lower your resting pulse rate. We'll raise your metabolism. We'll tone those muscles, tighten that belly, firm those arms. . . ." His eyes rested covetously on each part of her body as he named it.

"Now wait just a minute!" Phoebe shook her head, confused. "Just a cotton pickin' minute here. I . . . hey, watch it!" She put up her hands to catch the muffin Monk threw her. "What if it had dropped? Monk Brown, you'd better—"

"Good reflexes." Monk took a huge bite from another muffin and spoke around it indistinctly. "If you do good in your workouts I might teach you to juggle. C'mon, let's go."

Phoebe dug her heels in stubbornly, foiling his attempt to drag her across the floor. "In case you haven't noticed, I've got my nightgown and bathrobe on. Plus I have two children to feed and get dressed, not to mention the boarders—"

Monk let her go and scanned the kitchen shelves until he'd found a basket. He lined it with a clean dish towel, dumped in the muffins and presented it to her with a bow. "Voilà! The muffins are served. I'll dish oatmeal up for the kids while you jump into your sweats. You'll be finished with your exercise before cartoons are over."

In the end, of course, she gave in. The boys were delighted to have Monk give them oatmeal, along with extravagant stories about his past exploits as mime and acrobat. While he held them spellbound, Phoebe scrambled through the laundry basket for her exercise clothes. She put them on and looked in the full-length mirror that was hidden on the back of her bedroom door. The soft knit of the sweatpants and T-shirt seemed to hug every bulge.

Grimacing, she pulled on a shapeless cardigan and followed Monk out to his rickety VW bus. "Where are we going?"

"To Ross's club." He dangled a key in front of her. "It's not open Sunday morning, so you'll have a whole health club to yourself."

With you there, too, she added silently. They would be alone—no houseful of people around to chaperon.

But whatever she had feared or hoped would happen didn't occur.

It was less mortifying for Phoebe to pant and sweat without all those beautiful bodies in beautiful exercise clothes surrounding her. She found Monk's explanation of metabolic set points fascinating and illuminating. Her sore muscles eased as she stretched them under his direction, and the strange and complicated steps of the dances seemed simple when he demonstrated them for her alone. Best of all, her renegade desires sank to the back of her mind, and she concentrated on what she was doing.

"You have to relax," Monk told her as she sat spread-eagled on the mat, cooling down after the dancing. "Tense muscles get hurt. Just relax and hold the stretch. Don't bounce around like that."

Obediently Phoebe tried to relax. It wasn't too hard, because her whole body felt as if it wanted to collapse in a heap. She breathed as Monk instructed her to, and slowly a warm glow began to bathe her. She smiled dreamily up at him. "I feel great! Is this the exercise high I've heard so much about?"

He echoed her smile, and she felt their eyes link together, taking them down a swirling tunnel of sensation. Then he blinked and broke away, moving over to the barre. "I doubt it," he said huskily, clearing his throat. "That usually doesn't come until you've been working out for some time. Probably it's just the cessation of pain that feels so good to you."

"Probably," Phoebe said in a small voice. "Monk, what are we going to do?" she burst out, staring at him helplessly.

He gripped the barre in his hands as if he would break it. "I don't know." He cleared his throat again. "You are arousing some very. . . powerful things in me, whether you mean to or not."

"I don't know what I mean," she admitted. "But . . . I barely know you, after all. And then there's Tanner—"

She meant to explain that Angie's urging was what had made Tanner's letter seem so important. But Monk didn't wait to hear her out. "Ah, yes, the famous Tanner," he said bleakly. "I'll just have to manage to stifle myself. Wouldn't want to get in his way or anything."

"Monk, it's not like that at all!" But he didn't pay attention to her protest. He crossed to the mat and knelt in front of her, those amazing eyes fixed on hers earnestly.

"I said I'd help you, and I'll keep my promise." He took her hands absently in his, sandwiching them between his hard palms. "But not for Tanner. It's for you,

Phoebe, because you need to know how beautiful you are, and you probably wouldn't believe it unless you see it in the mirror." He clamped his lips together as if he'd said more than he meant to and got lithely to his feet. "So the next item on your physical fitness agenda is a low-calorie, nutritious breakfast." He smiled down at her. "Come along, Ms Sullivan."

PHOEBE WAS CURLED UP in the shabby armchair, trying to concentrate on the Sunday paper. Her mother had gone birding again, and the boys had mysteriously disappeared soon after helping with the noon dishes.

She stared blankly down at the newspaper in her hands without seeing a word that was printed there. All she could see was Monk, his eyes like crystal fire. All she could feel were the sensations he'd brought to her body, sensations that had been absent since Danny's death.

Danny would have liked Monk. By now he would have learned to juggle, she was sure. A tender smile touched her lips. Danny's enthusiasms had always had something childlike about them. He'd been a big brawny Irishman, with an exuberant spirit and a dreadful habit of procrastination. Their lovemaking had been tender, exciting, satisfying. She had missed it most in that first terrible year. But not as much as she'd missed the great gusts of his laughter or the warmth of his sleeping body next to hers. Danny had been familiar, someone she'd known as a friend before he became a lover.

There was nothing so easy about the feelings Monk created in her. He made her feel . . . wanton and desirable and special. It had been a long time since she'd felt like that.

She pressed her hands to her hot cheeks and tried to pull her thoughts out of the bedroom. There was more to any relationship than sex—hadn't she found that out with Tanner years ago? She and Monk appeared to share a mutual attraction. But their feelings would have to be far deeper than that before she could make love.

Firmly she picked up the paper and started to read. The headlines made no sense until she realized she was looking at the sports section. "Arrgh!" She tossed the paper aside and gradually became aware of thuds and treble screams of excitement coming from her backyard.

Curious, she investigated and saw half the neighborhood gathered in her muddy yard, watching enthralled as Monk rode around on a unicycle.

It soon became apparent that he was not merely entertaining. He jumped off the unicycle with a flourish and presented it to a gangling teenager who lived three houses down. "Come on, Bobby," he said encouragingly. "You almost had the hang of it before. Just use your arms for balance like I did."

Bobby Newton swallowed, his Adam's apple jumping in his long skinny throat. "Sure, Monk." His voice went up and slid back down again. "It doesn't *look* hard."

He managed to make it halfway around the circle of interested faces before he fell off. Then his sister Marlene pushed forward to try her luck, and the smaller kids, spearheaded by Jamie, began to clamor for a turn.

Phoebe stood behind the screen door, watching Monk in the circle of kids. Bobby Newton was taller than Monk by a couple of inches, but no one in the crowd was more than eighteen. Yet Monk treated them to the same interest and enthusiasm he gave the members of the aerobic dance class. With everyone else he shouted encouragement to Marlene, and when she had made a shaky circuit of the yard he made sure the younger kids got turns. The ones who fell off right away were allowed another try, and the ones who made it all the way around were given big rounds of applause.

Phoebe turned away from the screen door and found J.S. ambling into the kitchen, garbed in his natty maroon brocade dressing gown, with impeccable burgundy-striped pajamas showing around the edges. "What's all the whoopin' and hollerin' goin' on outside?" His sleep-creased face and sleepy mumble were in contrast to his immaculate appearance. "A man cain't get a decent day's sleep in this house."

Phoebe leaned against the sink counter and watched him rummage in the refrigerator. "It's midafternoon, J.S. Practically evening again."

He poured a big glass of milk and took a piece of fried chicken from the bag of dinner leftovers. "Landlady, it ain't evening until I says it is." Phoebe started laughing, and he watched her sourly. "What's so funny?"

"You are." She grinned at him. "You with that cornpone accent. You know your mamma didn't bring you up to talk like that."

J.S. looked sheepish, an expression only the thought of his mother could bring to his face. "Lordy, she'd wham the lights out of me if she caught me." His mother had made one memorable visit to Kirkwood from her snug little house in Afton. "She hates this earring, y'know." He reached up to finger the little hoop of gold in his left ear. "Plus she thinks I'm demeanin' myself, playin' jazz instead of that Van Cliburn stuff she raised me on."

"Better not let her catch you slanging like that, then."

Another loud roar from the backyard made J.S. straighten and put down his nearly denuded drumstick. He stalked to the back door and peered through the screen. After a long moment he turned back, looked pityingly at Phoebe and shook his head. "You in big trouble, Landlady. That man's gonna *get* you."

Phoebe fidgeted by the sink. "I don't know what you mean." J.S. laid the chicken leg down once again, and she added hastily, "I don't want to know, either." She watched a couple of bites disappear and couldn't restrain herself any longer. "Why does it qualify as trouble?"

J.S. waved the chicken bone. "Depends on your point of view," he said. "Now, from my point of view, this here setup is nigh on perfect. That dude cops you, and everthin' changes." He smiled winsomely. "You got us, Landlady. You don't need that clown."

Phoebe had to laugh. "I didn't know you were so self-centered, J.S. And your mamma tells me you're so sweet that rain is a hazard for you!" She turned as the back door groaned and Monk came in, ushering her muddy, beaming sons.

"We roded a *unicycle*!" Brendan screamed.

"I only fell off three times!" Jamie pranced in his excitement, and a few blobs of mud fell off him to splatter on the floor.

"Uh-oh." Monk looked apprehensively at Phoebe and pushed the boys back onto the small porch. "Scrape some of the mud off, and I'll see if I can rummage up a washcloth."

Both boys protested mechanically but obeyed. J.S. was cutting himself a piece of gingerbread with a cynical expression, and Phoebe left him in the kitchen and went to find a washcloth and some clean clothes for the boys.

Monk followed her across the hall and halted in the doorway. He hadn't seen the family quarters of the house yet. He looked around, not bothering to disguise his interest. Everything about Phoebe interested him.

The front room had originally been a parlor, he decided. Now it was someone's bedroom—Phoebe's at a guess. In one corner was a white wrought-iron bedstead with a bright comforter drawn primly up to the ruffled pillow shams. Broad casements, diamond-paned at the top, overlooked the front veranda. Set before the window was a big old table, its surface hidden by orderly piles of paper and a battered typewriter.

Around the walls there was a haphazard collection of bookcases, literally overflowing with books. An armoire and matching bureau flanked the bed. The large gracious room absorbed the unlikely jumble of furniture without a lessening of dignity. The effect was cluttered and somehow feminine and charming.

Through a connecting door he saw Phoebe kneeling before a battered chest of drawers, taking out clean jeans and shirts with swift efficiency.

The boys' room had been meant for a study or library, and its walls were covered with built-in bookshelves. Now toys and stuffed animals marched gaily along the shelves, as did an abundance of books and games. Pictures painted by the children were thumbtacked crookedly alongside framed Mother Goose prints and bright graphics. Monk saw a big Forest Service poster that portrayed assorted birds.

There was another room beyond this one. Catching the direction of his glance, Phoebe volunteered, "That's Mother's room." She shut the drawers and stood with the pile of clean clothes clutched to her chest. "We had the door cut through when I started the boardinghouse. It used to be the maid's room, I guess. Opened off the kitchen."

"Where did you sleep before that?" Monk forced the words out with some semblance of lightness. He could feel her resistance and knew if he didn't deal matter-of-factly with the past now, it would haunt them. "Where did you and Danny sleep?"

He watched compassionately as she gulped, but he wouldn't let her turn the question away. "Actually," Phoebe said, her voice low, "our bedroom was the room Edith has. I used your room as a sewing room, and the boys were in the other two bedrooms. We kept our books in here. The parlor that joins the dining room was Danny's goof-off space. We kept junk in the room Mother sleeps in, and what is now my bedroom was the living room." The look she gave him was resentful, but he tried not to mind. "Anything else you'd like to know?"

He followed her into her bedroom and moved swiftly to block her when she would have gone into the hall. "Just one more thing. Is that the bed you had before he . . . died?"

Phoebe's face was stiff. "None of your business."

He tried to keep his own face expressionless. Shrugging, he turned away. But Phoebe had seen the flicker of vulnerability in his eyes. She grabbed his arm. "It isn't the same one. Mother has that bed now." She hesitated, then rushed on in full babble, more disturbed than she cared to admit by his expression. "My grandmother was a hoarder, you know. She loved to buy things at auctions. After she died, we found seven bedsteads taken apart and stored in an unused corn crib. We started refinishing them. Then when Danny was gone, I. . .I kept on with them in a kind of work frenzy, and when they were done, I took this one as mine."

His hand came up to cover hers where it rested on his sleeve. His voice was husky when he spoke. "Thank you." He tipped her chin up and looked into her eyes. "I know it was none of my business. But I also know I'll be sleeping with you in that bed. I don't want to share it with Danny."

She was held by the brilliance of his eyes. Slowly his mouth came down until it touched hers with melting softness, once, twice....

When his mouth released hers, she spoke with dreamy inconsequence. "You're so sure of yourself. What makes you think you'll know the feel of my bed?"

He hugged her briefly, his face wearing that look of hunger she had noticed before. "Just whistling in the dark, Phoebe, love. And hoping. Hoping very hard."

Shaken by his intensity, Phoebe brushed past him. But no matter how she tried to occupy her mind with children to be tended and chores to be done, Monk's words stayed with her.

5

PHOEBE INCREASED THE VOLUME on her ancient stereo and sashayed up the stairs, a conga line of one. She sang loudly to the music while she stripped the bed in Edith's preternaturally tidy room.

It was Wednesday—day five in what she had begun to think of as the "new regime." This morning, for a change, she'd woken up with no aches and pains. In fact, even after the obligatory session of early-morning torture—an essential part of the new regime—she had energy to burn for the weekly task of changing bed linens and cleaning bathrooms.

Edith's room still looked almost exactly as it had when she'd moved in. Phoebe glanced automatically at the bedside table to see what she was reading these days. The English writer Barbara Pym—perhaps that was why she'd asked for tea this morning instead of coffee.

The April sun poured in through the wide windows at the head of the stairs as Phoebe deposited the load of bedding and headed for J.S.'s room. Inured to the rigors of Wednesdays, he managed to be up and out of the house by nine o'clock, heading for a downtown café where jazz musicians were treated with respect and given lots of free refills on their initial investment in a cup of coffee.

Phoebe opened the curtains in his room—something that happened only on these occasions—and tossed the bedding out to join Edith's at the head of the stairs. She didn't try to straighten the clutter of sheet music, score paper and obscure magazines, since a previous attempt to bring order from chaos had only brought J.S. into the kitchen breathing fire and threatening imminent departure.

Angie's room was full of frilly little pillows and beribboned stuffed animals—the kind of decorating achieved by pubescent girls. Angie used her own sheets, smothered in eyelet embroidery. Phoebe had to move a couple of long-haired fake cats off the matching eyelet comforter before she could strip the bed. The overpowering scent of musk made her wrinkle her nose and depart in record time.

She had saved Monk's room for last. The night before at dinner, he had been indoctrinated in the behavior expected of him on Wednesdays. Angie had recited the terrible fate that would occur to any boarder who didn't vacate on bed-changing day. "If you're not gone when Phoebe gets to your room, you have to do it yourself," she'd told him in tones of horror. "No matter how late you came in the night before. Phoebe makes you wash your sheets and dry them and everything."

So Phoebe had known he wouldn't be in. But she hadn't expected him to take the sheets off for her, either.

Yet there they were, neatly piled on the bed. It was a small gesture, but it touched her.

She added his sheets to the mound in the hall, along with the towels from the upstairs bathroom, and made a huge bundle that she pushed gleefully down the steps. Having the house to herself was fun, a privacy she didn't often enjoy. Jamie was at kindergarten, Brendan at preschool and her mother at the grocery store. So she stood for a moment at the top of the steps, exulting in her newfound energy, and then guiltily, because she wouldn't let the boys do it, she threw one leg over the polished oak banister and slid down.

The trip was exhilarating, but she gained speed toward the end and hit the newel post with a crash that bounced her right onto the floor. Rubbing her bottom, she marshaled her mass of laundry into a manageable bundle. Still stepping in time to the music, she dragged the bundle to the back porch, divided it into loads and fed the first one into the washer.

With clean sheets from the catch-all closet next to the bathroom under the stairs, she went back up to remake the beds. Again she saved Monk's room for last, and when the sheets were on, she took a moment to look around.

He had managed to leave his unmistakable imprint on the room that had been so prim and proper while Miss Nesbit had lived there. His unicycle, polished to a high gloss, perched in one corner. Through the partially open closet door she could see the electric-blue gleam of a stretch-satin jump suit—his acrobat's costume, she guessed.

There was a box of greasepaint on the dresser along with a fake red nose. She tried the nose on, liking the automatic smile it brought to her face. She was tempted to add some color with the greasepaint but was stopped by the thought of how long it would take to get it off. Regretfully she replaced the nose.

Along the top of the low bookshelves under the window Monk had set out a collection of hats. There was a monstrous sombrero, a prissy bowler, a glossy top hat, a battered sailor hat, a disintegrating straw farmer's hat of enormous proportions and a jaunty fedora, unexpectedly colored red, white and blue.

And in a corner by the door was a box full of juggling impedimenta. Or at least that was what she imagined the gaily painted clubs, balls of different sizes and slender blackened batons to be. She picked up three of the smaller balls and hefted them experimentally in her hands. Her boys had been practicing with Monk every evening and had begun to walk through the house nonchalantly juggling little bean bags that he'd produced from somewhere. If they could do it... She tossed two of the balls into the air and then stood helplessly as they fell in front of her. It was harder than it looked.

She put the balls away and went back to finish making the bed. Tucking in the final blanket, she noticed that the binding was unraveling. That would never do. For some reason she wanted Monk to have the best of what her house could offer. She folded the blanket and went back down to the closet to look for a better one.

The closet took up half the under-stairs space. The other half was occupied by a bathroom that had been

Danny's first major project after they'd bought the house. In the years since Phoebe had helped him put up shelves, the closet had changed from an orderly place to keep spare linen to a jammed catchall. Sheets and blankets still occupied the most reachable shelves. But the bottom ones were filled with things that were too good to throw away but too worn to use, and the top shelves had collected a seldom-used miscellany that often threatened to spill over.

And now it did. To reach the spare blankets Phoebe had to maneuver delicately around boxes of pictures and old photo albums. One of the albums slipped and tumbled to the floor at her feet. The fall dislodged half the photos, and they cascaded around her. Cursing, Phoebe gathered the pictures into a heap and carried the whole mess into her room, dumping it on her worktable.

She found it there later, after finishing the housework. She started to sweep it away to get to the advertising copy beneath it, but one picture caught her attention.

It was an old photo from her college days. In it she was standing in front of an ivy-covered wall on the University of Missouri campus, laughing up into a young man's handsome smiling face. Tanner.

For a moment she was transported back to those heady, laughter-filled days when she and Tanner had been in love. Correction—when she had been in love with Tanner. He had been a lot of fun, she had to admit. Romance with him had seemed exciting, an adventurous, no-holds-barred approach to life that was enormously attractive. He had been the first to awaken the woman in her, the first to teach her to take delight in her female body.

Until the day she'd found him in bed with another woman. She had realized then that commitment was important to her—and that Tanner would probably never make the kind of commitment she had unconsciously expected of him.

Could he make it now? She swept the pictures out of the way and searched among the piles of paper on her desk for Tanner's letter. Dropping into the swivel chair, she read it through, smiling nostalgically at his use of an old nickname.

Dear Bee: I have to confess I've had you on my mind for a while now. Somebody told me that Danny died, and I wish I had contacted you then.

I know you must have changed. I've changed, too—in a thousand different directions—since the days we were together. But something about those days has kept you fresh for me.

I've wanted to call you so often, but I was afraid you'd hang up on me like you did after we broke up—probably the only woman in the country who would. So I'm writing first, to tell you that I'll be calling soon. Please don't hang up. Please let me talk to you. I want to undo all these absent years.

My production company has scheduled some on-location shots for an episode about foiling drug smuggling on Mississippi River barges. I'll be based in St. Louis for three weeks in June. I want to see you then. I know you're not the same Phoebe I fell in love with so long ago. But I'm not the same Tanner I was then—thank God! Bee, I know you have no reason to think well of me. But please let me show you how I've changed.

I'll be calling in the next couple of weeks to set a date to meet you this summer. Oh, those muggy Missouri summers! I can hardly wait.

Until then, yours as ever,
Tanner

The first couple of times she'd read it, Phoebe had found his letter immensely touching. Of course, he still hadn't called—that took some of the luster off. And somehow the phrases that had seemed so artlessly confiding now looked practiced, polished.

But it was hard to summon up the fierce indignation and betrayal she'd felt all those years ago. Now she could barely remember having hung up on him, though it had evidently made an impression on him.

She picked up the picture and studied Tanner's young, laughing face. He was handsome, that was certain. She would have to make a point of watching his TV show again. The last time she'd turned it on had been before all this voice-from-the-past excitement. At that time, even seeing her old college lover on the tube had not been enough to keep her attention from wandering. She'd absentmindedly begun to read a hilarious Edmund Crispin mystery and had forgotten about the TV until her mother came in and turned it off.

Phoebe tucked the photo inside the letter and put them in a drawer. She really couldn't confront the problem of Tanner until the thought of his handsome mature self looking at her pudgy mature self no longer drove her into a panic. With Monk's help she would get into shape. Then she would feel confident that she could face him as a peer, not as a flabby housewife anxious to recapture a youthful fling. . . . So strong was the tonic of Monk's admiration that she could even smile a little at her first panicked reaction.

Phoebe reached for her folder on Lindbergh Drug Store. Trying to get the information the owner wanted into one tiny advertisement was going to need all her attention. She had none to spare for the vexing problem of why Monk occupied her thoughts so persistently. Especially his lessons in kissing. . . .

"To work!" She shook her fist at her reflection in the window and bent over the typewriter.

"SCOOP AND TOSS. Keep it high! Now the other one. In the same plane, in the same... Never mind. Here. Now, scoop and toss. Watch out!"

Phoebe collapsed in helpless giggles. "Sorry. Is your eye okay?"

Monk blinked with dignity. "Certainly. It would never have hit me if I hadn't dodged." He picked up the little bean bag and tossed it back to her. "Try again."

Phoebe put up her hands to catch the bag, forgetting that each hand already held one. All three bounced harmlessly to the floor, and she dissolved in laughter again. "I can't do it! I just can't get the hang—"

"You should be ashamed of yourself," Monk said sternly, "to stand there and tell me you can't do something your four-year-old son has totally mastered!"

"Now that's a lie!" Hands on hips, Phoebe confronted him. "Brendan can barely toss two, and you know it. Although I will concede that Jamie is magnificent. What do you do, drill him half the night?"

"No need." Monk picked up the bean bags and approached her purposefully. "He practices a lot. Just like you're going to do."

Phoebe took the bean bags back with a long-suffering sigh. Monk had cornered her at a vulnerable moment, when the boys had gone to take their bath and the dinner dishes were done, the time when she enjoyed reading a magazine or just absorbing the peace. Learning to juggle was cutting into this free time in a decidedly unpeaceful way.

"This is too hard," she complained, but Monk ignored her. He stopped behind her, and she could feel his warm breath on her neck. Her body shivered into awareness.

"Just relax," he told her, his arms coming around to cup her hands. "I'm going to move your hands for you and show you how easy it is."

"Relax. Okay." She took a deep breath, wishing he weren't standing so close that he could hear her heart pound.

"Uh, Phoebe—let go of the bags."

She looked down and realized she had the bean bags in a death grip. Monk was trying to pry them away from her. "Okay. I'll relax. All right."

He hefted the bean bags, one in his right hand, two in his left. "Toss from the hand with two first." A bag sailed into the air. "Then toss from the right when the first one reaches the top of the arc." Another bag went up, and amazingly, Phoebe's hand caught the first one. "Then the third one from the left hand again, when the second one has reached the top of its arc."

He held her hands cupped above his, her palms receiving the bean bags, while without seeming to move at all, he guided the bags through the air. The room was quiet except for little smacks as the bean bags landed in her hands and the rather noisy sound of their breaths mingling.

Phoebe knew why she was breathing hard. Although Monk made no overt moves, the heat of his body behind hers and the warmth of his hands made every nerve ending she had stand up and salute. Her skin tightened with anticipatory goose bumps.

Surely, he must be feeling the same way. Experimentally she nestled farther back into his arms. One of the bags missed her upturned palm and hit the floor.

Emboldened, Phoebe moved her hips slightly. The other bean bags joined the first one, and Monk's arms came around her, crushing her to him with pleasurable fierceness. His voice in her ear hovered between laughter and passion. "You wretch! What are you trying to do to me?"

Phoebe shivered as his arms tightened around her waist, then his hands moved up till they rested perilously beneath her breasts. "I don't know," she admitted. "Whatever it is, you were doing it to me first."

He turned her gently and looked into her eyes. She felt confounded with the need for him to kiss her, and yet she wanted to draw back. The unfamiliar poignancy that raced through her was sharp, too dangerous to pursue.

The bathroom door slammed, and small feet raced heavily toward the living room. Phoebe moved out of Monk's arms with something akin to relief. "Story time," she said, not looking at him as she picked up the bean bags.

"You keep them." He put his hands behind his back when she held out the little bags. "Practice up, though. You're going to need to know how to juggle."

Puzzled, she met his eyes. They were blazing again with that crystalline fire that seemed to dart through her. Gulping, she managed to find her voice as her sons came tearing into the room. "I am? What for?"

"For our troupe, of course."

Jamie caught the word and puzzled over it. "Troop of Cub Scouts?"

"Troupe of circus performers."

Jamie started jumping up and down around Monk. "Are we going to have a circus? Elephants! Tigers! Horses!"

Brendan dredged up unclear recollections of the only circus he'd ever seen, at age two and a half. "Will it smell bad?" he asked doubtfully.

Monk laughed and knelt to talk to them. "No animals. The circus I'm talking about is like the European ones, where there are acrobats and mimes and funny skits." He looked at their crestfallen faces. "If we want animals, we'll have to be the animals ourselves! How would you like to dress up as . . . as chimpanzees?"

The suggestion was wildly popular, and only Monk's assurances that the circus wouldn't be happening for a while saved Phoebe from the immediate need to produce chimp costumes. After the excitement, reading from *Peter Pan* seemed pretty tame. It took longer than usual to tuck the boys into bed, for they were bubbling over with questions.

When Phoebe finally escaped into the living room, she was ready to pick a few bones with Monk on the subject of exciting small boys just before bedtime. But there was no opportunity to bring him to an understanding of his perfidy. Angie had taken possession of the living room to turn on the old black-and-white TV.

She was huddled close to it along with Elizabeth, while Monk, frowning, lounged in the background. "See!" Angie's voice was reverent. "I should bring down my color set so you could see how gorgeous his hair is."

Curious, Phoebe joined them. Fast-action clips sped across the screen, accompanied by frenetic theme music suggesting that life-or-death matters were at stake. A man raced over the sands of some unknown beach, a revolver in his hand. Then the same man in a tuxedo whirled around a dance floor with a beautiful woman in his arms.

It was the beginning of "Fortune's Soldier," Tanner's TV show. The credits came up over a close-up of his face, strong jawed and intent like some archetypal man of action—the big-game hunter, the taciturn private eye. She sat down, determined this time to pay attention.

To see on TV someone she'd known felt strange; it was hard to reconcile the reality of her life with the fiction on screen. That man couldn't really be Tanner, of course, or at least, Tanner was nothing like that stereotyped adventurer.

But no matter how artificial the show's premise was, the fact remained that Tanner, a man she had known—in every sense of the word, she told herself wryly—had worked to make that fiction. He had stood under those impossibly tropical-looking palm trees by that picturesque ocean. He had danced around dressed to the teeth with a woman who made even Angie seem lacking in estrogen. Somehow it just seemed unreal—that this man should be writing her letters, begging her not to hang up on him!

"—does it to you?"

Phoebe came out of her trance to find Angie regarding her expectantly. "Huh?" She blushed and glanced at Monk. He was watching her, his face inscrutable. But she thought his mouth looked tight.

"I said," Angie repeated patiently, "has his hair always been so light? You knew him before. What do you think?"

"I guess so," Phoebe said, turning back to the TV. Tanner—or rather the character he was playing—was sipping a cocktail at what appeared to be an embassy ball or some such glittery occasion. The woman who stood talking with him was sleek, coiffed and gowned and groomed with an almost ferocious intensity. The looks she gave Tanner were industrial strength. She could have melted safe doors at twenty paces.

Phoebe barely heard Angie clear her throat; another woman had joined Tanner at the embassy party. This one was tall, fair and haughty, wearing a dress with cleavage that didn't stop.

She jumped to her feet. "I can't tell," she stammered to Angie. "I...I've got an old picture of him in my desk. You can decide for yourself." Her primary motive was to get away from the mental torture involved in comparing herself to those women. But she caught a glimpse of Monk's face as she bolted from the room, and she realized that he attached special importance to her having Tanner's picture handy.

She closed the door of her room and stood against it for a minute, wishing there was some way to repair the damage and deciding that there wasn't. Any excuse she'd make would just sound lame. And anyway, why shouldn't she have Tanner's picture around? There were lots of pictures of friends and relatives strewn through the house. No reason why Tanner's shouldn't be among them. Defiantly she hunted up a frame with a faded color snapshot of one of her cousins and stuck Tanner's picture in over it.

When she turned to go out, she came face-to-face with her reflection in the mirror on the back of the door. There was no way to avoid it; she could practically make two of one of those women hanging on to Tanner. Stricken, she stared at her ragged hair, her ordinary face, her overflowing curves. What in the world had possessed Tanner to bother writing to her when he was surrounded by women who embodied every man's fantasy? No wonder he hadn't called. His letter must have been momentary madness.

She took the picture back into the living room and endured Angie's artless disappointment that it, too, was black and white. "Why don't you have anything in color around here?" she demanded.

"Patience, my child." J.S. stood in the doorway, draping a long silk scarf around his neck. "I have arrived in living color!" He threw open his overcoat and revealed a shimmery, flame-red tuxedo jacket with black satin lapels, worn above black satin trousers piped in red. Everyone in the living room blinked at the vision.

J.S. sauntered in, buttoning his overcoat again. "You could be clamoring to come with me and hear some immortal music, and instead you're making like couch potatoes."

Monk raised his eyebrows, and Phoebe interpreted for him. "Tubers—those who watch the tube."

He thought this over, his lips moving quietly. "Couch potatoes—right."

"J.S. holds strong views about TV."

"They've never asked *me* to be on," J.S. explained simply.

"Yeah, but here's Phoebe's old boyfriend beating up three people at once!" Angie's excited words brought everyone back to the television.

Elizabeth was the first to turn away . "He doesn't seem to have changed much." She had met Tanner in

Columbia while visiting Phoebe that first year of college. "I've got a new nature book to read. Good night."

Phoebe looked after her mother as she vanished across the hall. Elizabeth had never said anything against Tanner, but she hadn't been surprised when Phoebe had stopped seeing him. And now her very silence on the subject was eloquent. Frowning, Phoebe turned back to the TV.

Monk dug his hands deeper into his pockets and thought about going up to his room. Then he wouldn't have to stay and listen to Angie drool over Tanner's profile.

He watched Phoebe more than he did the TV. At least she wasn't drooling. She sat curled in a shabby armchair, a faint frown puckering her forehead. He had to fight to keep himself from gnashing his teeth.

It was easy to see that those video glamour girls had raised the level of her self-doubt to a new high. He resented that. Couldn't she see that those women weren't real? Even that chump Tanner preferred years-old memories of Phoebe to the women he met in Hollywood. Why couldn't she see that?

The lamplight gleamed on her hair and tipped her long lashes with gold. He could almost feel the satiny texture of her skin under his fingers. Her hands had seemed ridiculously small and soft in his when they were juggling. He wanted her back in his arms, close enough so he could see the green-and-gold lights that danced in her brown eyes. And instead she was sitting there, feeling that she had to compete with high-gloss bimbos who looked as if they needed someone to tell them whether it was day or night.

Could he make her forget about Tanner? Could he sweep her off her feet before the great star made his appearance? Monk considered the question, frowning. He knew she wasn't indifferent to him, and he realized suddenly that he wanted her to fall in love with him as he was doing with her. But the situation was complicated. Even if she returned his feelings, would she always believe somewhere inside her that she had chosen him because she wasn't good enough for Tanner?

The thought made his blood surge. He wanted to leap to his feet, smash the TV and carry Phoebe off to bed. Was he falling into the same trap, comparing himself with Tanner? "I'm a better man than he is, Gunga Din," he muttered under his breath.

"Shh!" Angie hissed, watching raptly as Tanner vaulted over an electrified fence without messing up his designer suit. "God, he's gorgeous!"

"'Beauty,'" said J.S., straightening his silk scarf, "'is in the eye of the beholder.' And I've beheld enough. So long, folks."

Monk wished he could walk out, too, but he didn't want to leave Phoebe under the influence of this TV demigod. So he endured the show stoically, keeping his arms tightly crossed over his chest to subdue the urge to get physical.

At last Angie switched off the set and moved dreamily to the door. "I can't believe that he's actually going to be here in a couple of months!" She looked at Phoebe imploringly. "You will bring him here, won't you? You will introduce us all to him?"

"If it's possible," Phoebe answered cautiously. "He may have forgotten all about me by the time he gets here."

Angie ignored such poor-spirited talk. "I'm going to meet Tanner Hayden," she sighed, and headed for the stairs. "I could give him a little kiss. Maybe he'd kiss me back. . . ."

Her voice died away up the stairs, and Phoebe and Monk were left to look self-consciously at each other. Monk took her hands and pulled her out of her chair.

"That guy has a lot of nerve," he said huskily, drawing her close and rubbing his cheek on her silky hair. "Why doesn't he content himself with those airheads and leave the real women alone?"

Phoebe smiled up at him, but he could see the doubt in her face. "I don't know what he wants to see me for. I'm not in the same class with the women on his show."

Monk hugged her fiercely. "You're miles above them," he told her, but he could feel her disbelief. Sighing, he let her go. "You'd better get some sleep. Exercise class starts early in the morning."

She hesitated. "Why bother? I'd need a whole new face and everything!"

Monk resisted the impulse to shake her. "You know what?" He kept his voice casual, but some of his anger must have penetrated. She looked nervous. "You've got to make up your mind who you're living your life for, lady. Is it for Phoebe Sullivan, terrific woman? Or is it for some creep who puts physical appearance ahead of everything else? I was under the impression that this Tanner clown was merely providing the impetus for you to do something you wanted to do for yourself—get into shape. If you're really just trying to make yourself into someone else . . ." He let the words hang there for a moment, then gave in to the need to pull her close again. "Ah, Phoebe, love, why do you do this to yourself? You've got everything you need to be a wonderful person."

She felt stiff in his arms, and he could tell he'd overstepped the line. She wasn't prepared to open herself so far to him—not yet. Sighing, he released her and turned to go.

"Uh, Monk . . ." Her voice was gruff. He didn't turn, but a smile spread over his face. "Thanks. I . . . I guess I was being a jerk."

"See you in the morning." He kept his voice casual, and was relieved to hear her answer.

"Sure thing."

He wanted to leap up the stairs three at a time but took them decorously. Inside his door he stood waiting until he heard her snap off the living room light. The door to her room opened and closed, and he shut his own door.

He moved about his room getting ready for bed, deep in thought. He would have to slow down with her. He would have to take the chance of leaving her free until after Tanner came. She was too real, too intelligent, to be trapped by a handsome, empty profile. She'd rejected the jerk once; she was sure to do it again. And then he could make her love him without Mister TV hanging over them for the rest of their days.

The rest of their days... He stopped unbuttoning his shirt and pondered those words. They felt right. Smiling broadly, he went to brush his teeth and never noticed how the rocking chair rocked gently in his quiet room.

6

"WE FOUND HIM! Mom, come quick! We found Rufus!"

The children's shrieks broke her Saturday morning concentration, so Phoebe pushed her typing chair away from the desk and stretched briefly before abandoning Thrifty City Hardware. She just had time to shove her files to the other side of the desk before Rufus bounded in, his vitality not at all affected by his absence of the past two nights.

"Good dog, Rufus! I mean, bad dog!" She put out both hands to fend off his giant tongue, but Rufus got her anyway with an enthusiastic swipe across her face, his paws on her chest, his tail dusting the desk where her files had been. "Where were you, you bad dog?"

"We found him at the park," Jamie shouted, excited by the return of his pet. "Some other kid had him on a rope, but we got him back!"

Phoebe groaned, foreseeing problems. Rufus had a habit of wandering off and attaching himself to any child whose parents would allow such a monster into their homes, then he'd find his way back again and break the hearts of his adopted families. If she was lucky, the most recent victim's parents would be thanking their stars that Rufus was gone.

"C'mon, Rufus!" Brendan was hanging around the dog's neck affectionately. "Wanna biscuit?"

Rufus barked once and dragged the adoring children in the direction of the kitchen. Phoebe smiled helplessly at the sight of the ungainly animal, whose tail meant havoc to any table in reach. He looked cleaner; his new family had evidently given him a bath. She shook her head as she pulled her typewriter back into place. That meant trouble. Once you bathed a dog of Rufus's size and energy, you felt you had a stake in him. An irate parent was due to show up before nightfall.

Well, she would worry about that when it happened. Meanwhile, the ad copy she was writing wasn't behaving properly at all. "Thrifty City—it's hardware heaven for your nuts and bolts needs." She looked at the words and frowned. No zap, no zing. She liked to infuse her ads with her own puckish sense of humor, which, she felt, made them stand out from the usual boring grayness of small-budget advertising. "What's two football fields long and full of heavy metal? Your Thrifty City Hardware Store!" Hmm. She crossed her eyes at the uncooperative words on the page and began to make up totally unusable slogans. "Thrifty City—when you need new nuts (and bolts). Want a good screw? Come to us at Thrifty City. There's nothing soft about our hardware."

The shrill sound of the telephone was a welcome interruption until she remembered that it was probably

Rufus's latest temporary family tracking her down. Nevertheless she hurried to the kitchen to answer it.

"Phoebe, darling!" Subconsciously she registered the faint hiss of long distance on the line. Not an irate parent, then. Even as she searched her memory for uncles and cousins the voice could belong to, she realized with a lurch of her insides that it was Tanner.

He sounded cheerful despite her tentative hello. "Bee, darling, you won't hang up on me this time, will you?" His assured, bantering voice gave her a contrary impulse to do just that.

"Depends on what you have to say." She kept her voice light, forcing down the irrational resentment that flooded her. Some trace of it must have come through in her voice, for he sounded concerned.

"I didn't wait too long to call you, did I?" There was a chuckle, and she caught a hint of uncertainty that melted her. "I was afraid the letter wouldn't be enough to pave the way. You have forgiven me, haven't you?"

His voice pleaded for reassurance, but for one of the few times in her life Phoebe paused to think before she spoke. "Tanner, it was all so long ago. We weren't married or even engaged. I wasn't the arbiter of your behavior—I'm not now."

There was silence for a moment. "You know," he said unexpectedly, "that's what I told myself at the time. I wondered why you made such a fuss over it. But I can see now that even though we made no promises to each other, I violated your trust." His voice deepened. "I've come to value trust. Out here, trust is bought and paid for, and you only get as much as you can afford."

Good line, Phoebe thought, wondering cynically how many times he'd used it. She could picture him leaning over a crisp linen tablecloth in some exclusive restaurant, murmuring the line to a beautiful, blasé woman. "That sounds like something out of your TV show," she blurted, reverting to form.

Tanner mumbled something she couldn't decipher. "So, Bee, I'll arrive in St. Louis the first week in June. Will you save time for me? I want us to get to know each other again. I want . . . well, I'd better wait until I get there to tell you."

"No need to do that." Phoebe was devoured by curiosity. But Tanner wouldn't say more, and after a few more anticipatory phrases he hung up.

Phoebe hung up, too, gradually becoming aware of the usual Saturday noises that surrounded her—shouts and barks from the backyard, loud banging noises from the front porch, the swish and hum of the washer. Feeling oddly deflated, she drifted over to the calendar and turned the pages until she reached June. In pencil she wrote "Tanner?" on the first Friday. Then she went to find out what was causing the loud banging noises.

Monk crouched by the balustrade where a couple of the slats had fallen out. He was busily mending the holes with new slats. He glanced up as she came out and smiled around the nails in his mouth.

"You shouldn't be doing that," Phoebe told him, struck by a vague sense of guilt. Here was Monk, taking her exercise program in hand, teaching her kids to juggle, fixing her porch, for heaven's sake, and she had just made a date with a TV star. For some reason it seemed . . . disloyal.

"I wanted to." Monk sat back and regarded his work with satisfaction. "I love carpentry, and I don't get the opportunity that often." He ran a hand along the peeling paint of the porch. "Maybe next weekend I'll scrape this off. We could paint when it gets a bit warmer."

"Why don't I take it off your rent?" As soon as she'd made the suggestion, Phoebe was afraid he'd be offended. But Monk merely rubbed his chin consideringly. "I mean, if you like fix-it work, I can find plenty for you to do."

He nodded decisively. "Fine. You give me room and board half price, and I'll be glad to fix up around the place a bit. Just tell me what you want me to do."

They sat together on the front steps, enjoying the weak warmth of the spring sun while they planned the renovation of Phoebe's house. She didn't mention her phone call. Tanner and everything about him still seemed insubstantial, like one of the fictions he perpetrated on TV.

Monk, on the other hand, was as real as the sunshine in which they sat. He didn't touch her; he wasn't even looking at her, but still the excitement of his closeness carbonated her bloodstream. But now it was comfortable, too; she knew suddenly that they were friends, no matter what happened in the future.

He turned to look at her, and his expression made her feel somehow shy. Only eight days ago he had moved into her rooming house—impossible that he could have become so important in such a short time! Yet suddenly she was no longer a widow struggling to keep her family going. She was a woman again, a member of the opposite sex. And her body was remembering what the opposite sex was for.

The wonder and joy of it touched her as she met his eyes. "I was just thinking," she breathed, "about us being friends. It . . . it's a good thought."

He held her gaze steadily, his own eyes kindling into luminescence. "I have a better one," he whispered. The flame in his gaze stabbed her with delight. Their hands met and clasped in a touch like sweet lightning. He bent closer slowly, and she lifted her head, her lips craving his.

Then a car door slammed at the curb, and they jumped apart. Phoebe blinked, disoriented. Monk had almost kissed her, a kiss that she knew would have put to shame anything that had passed between them before. She took a deep breath and scowled toward the street.

Parked in front of her house was an elegant and expensive sedan, and coming up the front walk was an elegant and expensively dressed man.

He was tall and assured, wearing some designer's idea of play clothes, his dark hair groomed to perfection. And from the way he advanced purposefully on Monk, Phoebe realized who he must be.

Monk's own reaction was the clincher. "Here comes trouble," he muttered.

The man reached them and let a smile appear on his face. "Merlin. I've tracked you down, you see."

"Yes, I see." Monk's voice was unenthusiastic. "Lance, let me introduce Ms Phoebe Sullivan, my landlady. Phoebe, this is my brother Lancelot."

Phoebe murmured a greeting to which Lance responded perfunctorily before turning back to Monk.

"Merlin, dear boy, can we go somewhere and talk?"

"Lance went to Harvard for his schooling. Can you tell?" Monk said conversationally to Phoebe. "That's one reason why I decided on Berkeley."

Lance looked annoyed, and Phoebe, reluctant to find herself in the middle of a family quarrel, scrambled to her feet. "It was nice to meet you, Lance. I've got to get back to my work now." She shook Lance's hand briefly and marched into the house.

From her desk she could see them on the front steps, although she could hear no more than the murmur of their voices. Spying on people was rude, but there was little privacy in a boardinghouse, and Phoebe had often been an inadvertent eavesdropper. Now she frankly abandoned the attempt to work and watched as the Brown brothers aired their differences.

That they were disagreeing was obvious. Monk leaned against the porch pillar, his hands in his pockets and an obstinate, closed expression on his face. Lance stood in front of him, his arms making sweeping, dignified gestures, his mouth shaping words with a deliberation that just missed looking pompous.

Angie zoomed into the room and joined Phoebe at the window. "I saw that hunk from the upstairs window. Who is he?"

It was one thing for Phoebe to watch what was happening in front of her own desk, and another thing for one of her boarders to deliberately seek out a better vantage point. But she kept the thought to herself. "That's Monk's brother, Lance."

"Wow!" Angie gazed enviously at the gleaming car. "And I suppose that Maserati is his?"

"Is that what it is?" Phoebe dismissed the car with another glance. It was nice, but the dynamics between the two brothers was more important. Ignoring Angie, she watched Lance throw up his hands in defeat and turn away. Angie muttered disconsolately when the Maserati drove away, and she ran back up the stairs, perhaps to wait for Monk so she could find out if his brother was single.

Phoebe half got out of her chair when she heard the front door bang behind Monk. She thought he might come looking for her, but she didn't know if she wanted him to find her. Her emotions had been in turmoil since the interrupted kiss. She had wanted that kiss, had invited it, had even been conscious of a desire deep within her that it should lead to more.... The memory of Monk telling her that he wanted into her bed coursed through her body like a flash fire.

But the game seemed changed somehow. Before, she had been conscious of Monk as a man who awoke her femaleness, who wanted her and made her know it. Now she knew him, and knowing him, liked him. Wasn't it foolish to compromise friendship, perhaps a lifelong friendship, for sex?

Her body a confusion of desire and bewilderment, she waited for Monk to open the door to her office-bedroom. Instead, she heard the steady rhythm of his feet going up the stairs to his room.

She should have been glad to put some space between them. But she wasn't.

PHOEBE REMOVED the week's leftovers from the refrigerator, muttering to herself. "Angie's going out, J.S. has an early gig, that makes six...." She lined the containers up on the counter and took off the lids. Half a cup of beef Stroganoff, a pint of lentil soup, some macaroni and cheese, a burrito with two bites out of it and assorted vegetables. She dumped everything but the burrito into a big pot and added a jar of chicken stock out of the freezer then put the pot on the back burner to simmer. A handful of barley from the pantry, a few snips of parsley from the pot on the windowsill, and Saturday night supper was well underway.

She got out the ingredients for biscuits, but her hands slowed as she mixed flour and baking powder. Monk located her there, her hands deep in a bowlful of flour, gazing into space.

He often found her in the kitchen like this, as she meditated during cooking. There was something of the ancient matriarch in her easy command of pots and pans, he reflected. Watching her, he could see that cooking for her family and her boarders was like a sacrament to Phoebe.

He had never known any woman like her before. It wasn't just that she was easy to be with, that he liked the way she laughed and her almost painful honesty. She had a much deeper, more unsettling effect on him, as if her femaleness spoke directly to his masculinity. He felt the need for her as a constant ache within him. His hand tightened on the doorframe when he realized how long it would be—if ever—before that need could be slaked.

Phoebe looked up and saw him, and he forced a pleasant smile to his face. She didn't know him well enough to believe that he felt what he did, and he didn't want to scare her by coming on too strong, too soon.

She returned his smile, a hint of sympathy in her expression. "So did he put you through the wringer?"

With an effort he remembered Lance's visit. "He tried." She glanced at his hands, and he noticed that they were balled into fists. Shoving them into his pockets, he wandered over to the stove and sniffed. "Smells great. What is it?"

"Soup." Phoebe smiled, that blinding, riveting smile that brought a flush of heat to his face. "Leftovers, actually. We often have soup or something goopy on Saturday to use up the leftovers. Why doesn't your brother want you to live here?"

Monk blinked. She certainly didn't beat around the bush. Then he saw that she was blushing, turning back to the mixing bowl. "Phoebe," he said gently, "you can say anything you want to me. Always."

"My. . . my desk does face the window," she stammered, "and I couldn't help but see . . ." The blush receded. "Anything?"

"Anything at all." He regarded her thoughtfully. "You couldn't hear us? Pretty perceptive of you to know what we were talking about."

"I could see his lip curling when he looked at the yard." Phoebe began rolling the biscuit dough. "Where does he live, Chesterfield?"

"Ladue," Monk admitted. "He has a place not that far from my parents', as does my sister." He watched the swift movement of her hands cutting out biscuits and arranging them on a baking sheet.

"He wants you to move to your folks' place," Phoebe said knowledgeably.

"It's more than that!" Monk's words burst forth, and Phoebe stopped working to stare at him. She was used to his equable temper. But now he began pacing between the sink and the table, his hands thrust deep within his pockets, his face dark with anger. "He wants me to go back to ball bearings. He wants me to climb meekly back into the vice presidency where I belong and stop playing around with this childish acrobat stuff."

Phoebe sat down at the table and propped her chin on her hands, watching him. She had not realized his feelings about starting his troupe ran so deep. She, like Lance, had figured Monk would eventually tire of the uncertain life and go back to his family's business.

Unlike Lance, however, she admired Monk for his plans. Too often people let themselves be trapped in a mold they hated because it was what was expected of them. If she had followed conventional wisdom after Danny's death, she would have found some secretarial job that barely paid for child care and food. She would have sold the big, shabby house she loved and got a small, practical place.

Instead she'd opened the boardinghouse to pay expenses and brought in the rest of the money she needed by work she found for herself. It wasn't uplifting to write about nuts and bolts for Thrifty City, but it paid the bills, and she had independence and control over her work life, neither of which she wanted to sacrifice for security.

"I had a job as a secretary once, just after I got out of school," she said, following her own thoughts. Monk stopped pacing and leaned against the sink, his arms folded tightly across his chest. "It wasn't my kind of thing at all. I don't make much money doing what I do, but the expenses are low, too. I mean, it's been three months since I had to buy a pair of panty hose."

Monk smiled and relaxed. "In my profession, I go through a lot of tights. But I get your point." He joined Phoebe at the table and sat for a moment, studying his clasped hands. "It's not that I'm not fond of my family," he said at last. "I am. But none of them understand. They feel it's a case of a grown man running off to join the circus." His eyes turned introspective. "It's not just that. I tried to limit my wardrobe to business suits, but something inside me needs to wear motley, too. I feel connected to humanity, to our common ancestry, when I make people laugh. But my family doesn't listen when I tell them all this. If I thought that by living at home for a while I could make them understand . . . but it wouldn't work, and I'd hate it!"

Phoebe let her breath out thankfully, only then realizing that she'd been holding it. *I don't want the kids' juggling lessons upset,* she told herself, not wanting to examine the real reason why she was so relieved that she wouldn't lose Monk as a boarder. "Maybe you could visit once in a while," she suggested generously, picking up the biscuits and sliding them into the oven. "Stay a weekend sometime."

Monk shook his head. "Better to keep away, since they're already used to my absence," he said. "Besides, I'm going to need the weekends. I met a couple of closet acrobats who work out at the Fitness Emporium, and they're interested in getting together, but weekends are the only time they have free."

He shoved his chair back and stood up, taking her hands when she would have walked past. "Phoebe," he said huskily, "thanks for listening. It means a lot to me."

"Oh, well . . . anytime." Phoebe wet her lips absently, wondering how to go about getting the kiss she'd almost had on the porch. She wanted that sweet feeling Monk's kisses gave her, and she knew he would never force her in any direction she didn't want to go. She looked up at him, trying to put her longing into her eyes, hoping he might read it there. *Please, Monk, I want you to kiss me, although I don't want any pressure about going to bed. I don't know what I want, but I want your lips. . . .*

Dreamily she heard the sounds of her house around her: the thick tick of the kitchen clock, the clunk of the warped old baking sheet settling in the oven, more distantly from the backyard the shrieks of the boys mingled with Rufus's loud excited bark. But here in Monk's arms it was still, as if they were wrapped in a magic circle that nothing could penetrate.

His arms tightened, and she closed her eyes, anticipating the touch of his mouth on hers. Their lips met, the gentle pressure sending a tremble of delight through her, sparking fires all over her body. Shivering, Phoebe gave herself up to the pleasure of Monk's kiss, meeting the escalating need of his mouth with her own hunger. Their tongues touched in the most delicate of caresses, then touched again and again, igniting a fierce heat that burned every place their bodies met.

Monk slid his hands under the loose sweatshirt she wore. His palms moved along the smooth flesh of her back, and Phoebe shivered again. She could almost feel the sensations he felt, as well as those he raised in her. Her skin seemed like satin under his hands. Nerve endings quivered and came to life beneath his fingertips.

Then his hand was on her breast, and she gasped at the sensations that flooded her. Her nipples budded erect at his gentle probing. The sound of his groan brought a flush of heat to her skin. Dizzily she let her own hands explore, sliding them over his back, down the tight curve of his jeans.

He groaned again and pulled her closer to him, his hands in the small of her back. "Phoebe, love, I want you. . . . You know I do—you know how much . . ."

The words, breathed in her ear, made her body react with an ancient instinct. She pressed herself delicately into the cradle of his pelvis. Yes, he did want her, and she wanted him, but—

Slowly she began to regain the common sense his kisses had ravished from her. With a sigh of regret she stepped away.

He released her reluctantly. "Phoebe?"

"Monk, it just won't work. How can I have an affair with one of my boarders? What kind of boarding-house would this be?"

His smile was ragged. "I'm not asking you to stage an orgy for my benefit, love. Can't we just go sedately to bed?"

Phoebe shook her head and turned away until she could fight down the sting of tears. "I live here with my mother and my kids, for heaven's sake. It...it just feels too inhibiting." She sniffed the warm kitchen air and picked up a hot pad.

Monk stood silently while she turned the sheet of biscuits in the oven so they would brown evenly. She put off looking at him until she could no longer fuss over the stove.

His face was shuttered, guarded, but he ran his hands through his hair, and she could see that his fingers trembled. "Do you want me to move out?"

"Oh, Monk!" Aghast, she dropped the hot pad. "Of course not! Why, we'd all miss you so much—"

"All of you?" His voice was still quiet, but there was a sharp edge to it she'd never heard before. "Phoebe, your kids are great, your mother is swell, but it's you I really care about." He watched her for a moment, but her throat was choked with emotion, and she couldn't speak. "Maybe it would be better if I left."

He took two distracted steps toward the dining room. Phoebe watched him and knew the tears were going to overflow. "Monk—" she whispered. "I thought we were friends!"

He stopped in the doorway, standing rigid, his back toward her. For one fathomless minute she thought he would go on walking. Then his shoulders slumped, and he turned to face her.

"We are friends," he said, the words coming from him with difficulty. "And maybe I can act like just a friend as long as I don't touch you." His eyes were bright with passion and torment. "But I won't make any promises about what might happen if you kiss me again."

Then he was gone. Phoebe sank into a chair at the table and stared at the space he'd occupied. She was heated, restless with desire, confused at the intensity of her emotions, and she railed at her stupidity in letting a few foolish scruples deny her the pleasure she knew would be found in Monk's arms.

By the time she remembered to take the biscuits from the oven, they were very well done indeed.

7

PHOEBE TURNED HER HEAD AWAY as Monk manipulated the scale's weights. "Two more pounds," he announced with satisfaction.

"Is that all?" She stepped off the scale and regarded herself critically in the big health club mirror. "Seems like it should be more, the way I have to keep tightening my belt." She pulled the drawstring of her sweatpants in a little more.

"You're replacing fat with muscle," Monk explained. "Muscle weighs more. Sometimes you can lose many inches and not a single pound."

He picked up his portable tape recorder and his hooded sweatshirt. Phoebe watched him surreptitiously. He wore a sleeveless black T-shirt with San Francisco Mime Troupe across the front, and old gray sweatpants. She thought he looked wonderful. His skin still gleamed from the exertion of the class they'd just finished, and his hair stood up in damp dark spikes where he'd pulled off the headband that kept the sweat out of his eyes.

He looked up and caught her watching him. Their eyes locked and held. Then he straightened and she turned away, blushing and self-conscious in front of the few class members who'd lingered to talk.

But no one had noticed the brief interplay between Monk and Phoebe. Angie was flirting outrageously with Ross, and John, the weightlifter, was already installed in one of the Nautilus machines. In fascinated horror Phoebe watched him flailing and flexing his bulging muscles as he pushed various parts of the machine.

"Ready to go?" Angie came over to her, jingling her car keys. She caught the direction of Phoebe's glance, and her eyes gleamed. "Some hunk, huh?"

Phoebe shuddered and turned away as Monk joined them, but Angie poked her in the ribs as they left the club. "Don't you think so? All those muscles! I love the way he wears those tight little shorts."

Phoebe shook her head as she climbed into the front seat beside Angie. "He doesn't do anything for me. I think his muscles look...obscene! Great writhing coils of . . . of meat!"

Monk, settling into the back seat, let loose a guffaw. But Angie frowned. "It's sexy as hell! I suppose you like the tubby ones, like Paul or Raymond."

"Uh-uh." Phoebe looked dreamily out the window. "I like those lithe, whippy ones." *Like Monk,* she added silently. *The man I've avoided being alone with for the past two weeks.*

"Tanner isn't built like that," Angie said, her voice casual. But Phoebe saw her eyes flick to the rearview mirror to gauge Monk's reaction. So she had noticed that there was something going on between Phoebe and her latest boarder. What Angie saw, the whole world soon knew.

It had been dangerous to agree to the juggling sessions in the backyard. Phoebe had told herself that with the boys there, not to mention assorted residents of the boardinghouse, it would be safe enough. And so it was—physically. But there had been too many moments like the one back in the club, when her eyes would meet Monk's and both of them would go off in a trance. Too many times when his hand would brush hers, and their hands would tremble. For the hundredth time Phoebe wondered what was the matter with her.

When the car pulled up, she scurried into the house as quickly as she could. For the next couple of hours she occupied herself with doing her morning chores: getting breakfast out of the way and the children off to school.

At last she was in her room, her feet propped up on her desk, the radio turned on low to facilitate thought. But instead of thinking up new copy for the drugstore, she found her mind filled with images of Monk. Sighing, she abandoned the attempt to work and let her thoughts go where they would.

There was no doubt she was attracted to Monk. She glanced toward the bed and pictured him there—sleek muscles and all. She went a step further and pictured him naked. The longing ache that rose in her was too intense. Alarmed, she sprang up and began to pace in the small area between the desk and her bed.

Why couldn't she just give in to it? Monk was ready and willing to do his part to ease the feelings she could no longer control. Why did she hold back from the pleasure he had to offer?

She paused in front of the full-length mirror and assessed what she saw there. She wasn't thin—she would never be thin. But the generous curves of the past month were somewhat tamed and controlled. Even though she had another month's worth of shaping up before her, she felt a justified pride in the improved body she saw in the mirror.

"I'm *saftig,*" she announced to the person in the mirror. "Pleasingly fleshed." Looking at that body, she no longer felt too fat and unattractive for romance—which was a good thing, because she was sure Tanner had romance on *his* mind. She glanced at the corner of her desk where a big mason jar squatted, crowded with roses. There were roses in every corner of the house, sent two times a week by courtesy of Tanner. Phoebe had no illusions that he personally selected the flowers. But the gesture was a telling one.

So if she could contemplate romance with Tanner, why couldn't she do so with Monk? Phoebe resumed her uneasy pacing. From the moment she'd got Tanner's letter she had imagined scenarios of their meeting. They differed in detail, but most of them had in common a dimly lit setting, a suddenly glamorous Phoebe, a properly smitten Tanner. She knew, of course, that it was so much daydreaming. But that didn't matter. The whole situation was straight out of a daydream, so the unreality of her expectations didn't trouble her.

But with Monk—ah, no getting away from reality there. There was no suddenly glamorous Phoebe possible for the man who'd watched the excess pounds leave her body. The feelings he roused in her were too sharp, too vivid, for fantasy. Reality couldn't be manipulated as fantasy could. Before she could let herself be swept away by it, she would have to be more sure that it would take her where she wanted to go.

"Disengage mind from erogenous zones," she commanded herself, sitting down at her desk. "I have to think." Her fingers drummed lightly on the keys of her old manual typewriter. The truth was, she was confused. Terribly confused. Somehow to her fevered brain it seemed that a kiss from Monk would make everything well again.

And on that thought, she saw Monk push her door open and come in. He stood for a moment looking at her soberly then shut the door behind him.

Her mouth went dry. As he eased one lean hip onto her desk, she knew he'd come to "have it out." He looked so good.... He'd had a shower, as she had. As usual he had combed his hair with his fingers. Her own fingers longed to ramble through the dense, furry mat, especially the part at his temples where a sprinkle of silver resided. He was wearing a rugby shirt and well-worn jeans that clung with loving softness to the sleek muscular lines of his thighs.

Phoebe felt her chest expand and wondered at her difficulty in breathing. It was just Monk, she tried to tell herself. No reason to get excited.

"We can't go on like this." Monk's words burst out, and he ran his hands through his hair again. "Phoebe, I'm going crazy. I know what I told you, but I take it back. Can we have some of those kissing lessons again?"

Phoebe smiled tremulously. "Oh, Monk. Are . . . are you sure it's wise?"

He grabbed her hands and hauled her up to stand between his legs. "Of course not," he growled, pulling her closer. "It's the dumbest thing I ever did. But I can't stop myself from falling in love with you, no matter how much I try. So maybe this way I can make you fall in love with me."

His mouth came down on hers with none of the gentleness and patience she remembered from their earlier kisses. This time it was a pent-up explosion of the desire they'd both tried to keep in check. She melted against him, liquefied by the hot sweet fire that swept through her. Disdaining any delicate love play, their tongues met and strained for more closeness. His hands were everywhere, urging her to full arousal.

Phoebe gave in to the increasing need to touch him. She swept her hands down his lean flanks then up again, brushing against the hardness she found there, then repeated the caress with more pressure.

"Phoebe, my God!" Monk tore his mouth away, his chest heaving. With a vague sense of detachment Phoebe noticed her own lungs were having trouble finding air. "Do you know what you're doing? Do you know what I want to do?"

Phoebe looked into the blazing blue crystal of his eyes and was lost. "I know," she mumbled. "I . . . I want it, too."

She never knew how she landed on the bed. She was just there, and Monk was there, too, his shirt already off. He cradled her in one arm as he undid the buttons of her shirt with shaking fingers. She ran her hands lovingly over the smooth tanned skin of his shoulders as she had wanted to do for so long. He shivered under her touch, and she found herself languidly kissing and nipping at the taut muscles of his chest.

The sound of his tormented groan was like heartwood to the fire that burned her. He finished undoing her shirt and laid it open, then fumbled with the catch of her bra. In another minute he'd disposed of that, too. Then he caught her close, her breasts crushed into his chest, and their bare skin warmed each other.

"Phoebe, love," he whispered into her ear, his breath uneven. "I want to make love to you—so badly, my love. But I'll stop . . . whenever you say."

"Don't stop." The fever inside her was so hot, so high. The idea of not assuaging it was ridiculous. "I want you, Monk, I want you so much—"

He kissed her again, this time not so ruthlessly. His lips were tender, so indescribably sweet that it was hard to believe they could heighten the need within her so swiftly. When he took his mouth away she cried out her loss and opened her eyes. He was looking at her naked torso, her flushed cheeks and heavy eyes, with fierce satisfaction on his face.

"I've been dreaming of this for so many nights," he growled, sliding his palm across her shoulder and down to cup the fullness of her breast. He bent to kiss each rosy crest, his eyes drifting shut again. "Ah, you taste so good . . . just as I thought you would. . . ."

Phoebe moaned as his hands and mouth played across her breasts, bringing new peaks of pleasure with every caress. But she wanted more, she needed more than the touches that drove her mad, more than the waves of desire that intensified every minute. . . . At last she pressed his head to her breast, whispering his name fiercely. "Monk, Monk, I need you—"

He laughed exultantly and his caresses changed. Using his teeth he nipped lightly, erotically, at the rosy crests until she was moaning, writhing. She felt his hand at her waistband and arched her body with instinctive invitation. He unzipped her jeans, but she couldn't wait for him to pull them down. She wanted those clever hands all over her body, especially the places that tormented her with heat. Shamelessly she grabbed his hand and showed him where the need was greatest.

Somehow she must have unzipped his jeans, although her swirling thoughts held no memory of it. But she was grasping him intimately, glorying in the strong thrust of what she held, knowing that there could be more but unable to wait, because lips, fingers, everything was spiraling out of control. . . .

Then the back door slammed, and Elizabeth's voice called out, and Phoebe, fond of her mother though she was, said with great force, "Damn and blast!"

She began scrambling into her clothes, muttering under her breath, "She'll be here in a minute, she'll be so embarrassed—"

Monk grabbed her arm, stilling her frantic movements. "Are you sure," he asked, his voice level, "it's not you who's embarrassed?"

Phoebe stared at him, doubt and anxiety flooding her. This was not romantic—to be tumbled in the bedclothes, in fear of discovery from her mother, and at the age of thirty-two instead of seventeen. "Maybe I am, a little," she acknowledged. "But not because of what we did—and what we almost did." The memory of that pleasure filled her with a shy ecstasy. "Mostly I guess I'm frustrated."

"Me, too," Monk muttered fiercely, closing one hand over her breast in a strangely pagan, claiming gesture. His touch brought back all the passionate languor of a few moments before. He squeezed, and she caught her breath. Then he crushed her to him before he abandoned her to roll off the bed.

"If you keep looking at me like that," he said, his voice sounding strained, "I won't be responsible for what your mother finds." He turned away, zipped his jeans and pulled on his shirt.

Phoebe finished buttoning her own shirt and jumped off the bed. Elizabeth called again, and now she could understand the words. "Come help carry in the groceries!"

Smoothing her hair with trembling hands, she went toward the door. Monk pulled her against him, pressing her for an instant into his waiting hardness. "Phoebe, when?"

She let her fingers creep through the silk of his hair. He was falling in love with her. "As soon as possible." As if it hadn't just been partially placated, her body was clamoring again, sending those fire alarms to every nerve ending. *Warning, warning, control the blaze.*

Monk released her after one hard, searing kiss and followed her out of the room. Behind them, some errant breeze sent the curtains into a flurry of movement.

HER MOTHER WAS at the back door, field glasses in hand, as they entered the kitchen. "It's the most amazing thing," she said distractedly, sweeping the nearby treetops with her field glasses, "but I thought I saw a European goldfinch when I pulled into the drive."

Phoebe sidled past her mother and headed for the back of the old Volvo sedan. Monk followed her, and she loaded his arms with grocery bags. They exchanged one helpless, burning look, and then Phoebe turned away to trudge back to the house with her share of the groceries.

Elizabeth was on the phone in the kitchen. "Yes, I'm positive," she said, fixing her eyes on Phoebe with absentminded ferocity. "I couldn't mistake that face pattern."

Phoebe stood at the pantry, taking the bags of flour Monk handed her and putting them away. He gave her a sack of lentils then grasped her fingers tightly when she reached for the peanut butter. She felt her face go scarlet and railed at her own lack of self-control. Glaring, she snatched her hand away.

Turning back to the kitchen, she saw that the absentmindedness had left her mother's face. Now Elizabeth looked from Monk to Phoebe, and speculation was evident in her gaze.

"Impossible, Cynthia," her mother snapped, her attention once more on the telephone. "Bring your binoculars over tomorrow morning, and we'll just see whose eyes are getting weak."

Muttering, Elizabeth stalked out the back door. Monk and Phoebe were left alone in the kitchen, but Phoebe at least was painfully aware that another interruption was bound to occur. So she resisted the impulse to go to Monk and wind herself wantonly about his body. She thought about bringing up the subject of love. *Say, Monk, about love—do you think of it as ephemeral in nature, like the first flowers of spring, or more enduring? And which of these do you feel for me?*

It was no use. She couldn't fish for his love like that. But she had heard him say it. She hugged that to herself. Of course it could have been a line to get her into bed. She knew that Tanner's protestations of love a decade earlier had been meant for just that purpose. But she didn't feel that Monk would stoop to using a line.

Feeling the silence heavy between them, she reached out to the radio that perched on a shelf above the sink and snapped it on. A blast of frenetic drumming and shrieking guitar made her wince. She started to change the station, but the music ended abruptly in a commercial.

Monk began to speak, but she hushed him quickly, a delighted smile on her face. "This is my Thrifty City spot," she hissed, one ear cocked to the radio. "It turned out pretty well."

The spot was a tiny radio drama. An insolent punkish voice answered the clerk's polite "May I help you?"

Punk: Yeah. Where's the heavy metal?

Clerk: Do you mean the chains or—

Punk: I'm lookin' for a stainless-steel vest.

Clerk: I think you must have the wrong place. This is the Thrifty City Hardware Store.

Punk: That's what I'm lookin' for—some hard wear. Got any iron stocking caps?

Clerk: I . . . I don't know. We have everything for anyone's hardware needs—nuts, bolts, pipes, joints—

Punk: Oh, yeah? I didn't know you could sell that stuff in a store.

Clerk: —lumber, fencing, garden equipment—

Punk: No stainless-steel vests?

Clerk: Uh . . . no.

Punk: Oh, well—you said chains?

Clerk: Certainly. A fine selection of chains—steel, aluminum, copper—right this way. (Sounds of rattling chains)

Punk: Wow, these are evil, man! I think the copper is *me*.

Clerk: Looks great. Hey, doesn't your head ever get cold, all shaved like that? No?

The characters' voices faded into a voice-over that gave the Thrifty City pitch. Phoebe turned the volume down and looked complacently at Monk, who laughed with delight. "Great ad!" He wiped his eyes on his sleeve. "Does it sell hardware?"

"It seems to work pretty well on the youth-market stations." Phoebe handed Monk a paper towel. "They have conventional ads for the more sedate stations. But the new Thrifty City owner told me that he wanted something that would grab the attention of young people."

"Well, that should do it." Monk tossed the paper towel in the trash and looked at her curiously. "You have a real flair for it, don't you?"

She looked at the floor, pleased and a little embarrassed. "I don't know how to take compliments," she said gruffly. "If that was one."

"It was." Monk reached for her hand and swung it gently. "Say, instead of taking my handyman work out of my room and board, why don't we make a new deal? I'll fix up around the house, and you write me a skit for my troupe."

Intrigued, she looked up. "What kind of skit?"

Monk let her hand go and began to wander around the kitchen. She could tell that thoughts of romance had been replaced with concern for his act. "It would have to be in mime," he said finally. "No dialogue."

She gulped. "That makes it hard."

He perched on the table and stared at her meditatively. "It's all visual in that type of performance, you see. Dialogue is difficult to put across in those surroundings. You want something funny, poignant, archetypal, captivating, memorable. . . ."

"No sweat." Phoebe stared at him. "Really, Monk, don't ask the impossible or anything."

"You can do it," he told her, reaching for her hand once again. "You can do anything."

PHOEBE SAT on the back porch steps. Laura and Jim, the latest additions to Monk's troupe, sprawled below her in the warm May sunshine, dressed in gorilla costumes, the hairy heads in their laps. Jamie and Brendan buzzed around awestruck, fingering the costumes until Phoebe made them sit, one on either side of her, and wait for the show to start. As was usual lately on Saturday afternoons, a motley collection of neighborhood children stood around between the house and the old run-down garage.

Monk stood at the far side of the practice ring he'd set up in the yard, his back to the audience. In honor of the skit Phoebe had written for him he wore a shabby old tuxedo tailcoat and a loud deerstalker hat he'd dug up out of his collection. He also carried an outsize magnifying glass.

He turned and advanced toward the audience, a vacuous, amiable grin on his face, the magnifying glass held up before him. Then he began to trip over things he'd produced from the hidden pockets of his tailcoat and examined pompously under the glass—a rubber chicken, an enormous shoe, a giant-size pair of polka-dot drawers that drew guffaws from the children and, of course, a banana in all its manifestations from fruit to peel. The pratfalls escalated from simple sprawls on the ground to elaborate flip-flops.

Then, scrutinizing the ground through his glass, Monk picked up something before tripping on it—a dainty lace handkerchief. Smitten with love, he sniffed the delicate fragrance, admired the lace, pressed the token to his heart while rolling his eyes heavenward. He looked for the owner of the handkerchief everywhere—under leaves, behind trees, even in all his pockets.

Laura and Jim got up and put the costume heads on. Laura's gorilla wore a flirtatious hat with an eye veil, and white lace gloves on its hairy black paws. Jim's gorilla had a homburg and a briefcase.

The female gorilla minced into the center of the "ring." She sauntered past the searching Monk, then stopped and snatched the handkerchief. The detective, appalled, snatched it back. Simpering with the handkerchief held to her face, the gorilla struck a maidenly pose.

Realizing that this was the one to whom the handkerchief belonged, Monk got down on one knee, taking off the deerstalker hat. He waved his arms around in impassioned declaration. The female gorilla listened to him, but when she caught sight of the male gorilla carrying his briefcase, she stopped paying attention to Monk.

He got to his feet and tried to take her in his arms, but she pushed him away (another pratfall) and dropped the handkerchief in the male gorilla's path. He picked it up, they linked arms and strolled happily away together.

Monk was disconsolate. His shoulders slumped, his magnifying glass drooped. Pacing with his head down, he didn't notice Marlene Newton until he ran into her.

Marlene was also wearing a shabby tuxedo jacket and a deerstalker hat, but her hat had a big red bow on top of it. She gazed at Monk, he gazed at her, and both turned toward the audience with their hands on their hearts. Holding hands, they did simultaneous leaps and clicks of the heel offstage, which was behind the garage.

The audience clapped and cheered, and Laura and Jim came back, already climbing out of the gorilla suits. "These things are hot," Laura grunted, hopping on one foot while she tried to pull the other one out of the costume.

Monk took off his deerstalker and gave Phoebe an exuberant hug. "I knew you'd write something great. It went really well, and the gorillas were an inspired thought."

Phoebe smiled sheepishly. "Actually, I asked Laura what costumes she had access to at the community theater. Gorillas were on the list so I used them."

The children crowded around, wanting to try on the gorilla outfits, but Monk distracted them by starting juggling practice. Soon the air was filled with flying objects. After watching for a few minutes, he came back to the porch, where Phoebe was being helped into one of the costumes by Laura.

"These are good costumes," Monk said, examining the head of the other gorilla. "Look how well this is made, with the teeth and all."

Phoebe, inside the female gorilla, gnashed her teeth at him. It was bizarre to be inside the costume, looking out through the mask that totally covered her head. Laura and Jim turned away in a technical discussion of the flip-flops Monk had done, and he pulled the other gorilla mask over his head and approached Phoebe.

"Want to monkey around?" His voice was muffled by the mask.

"Sure, honey." She made kissing noises and brought her face close to his then jumped up and down emitting what she hoped were gorilla grunts.

"Hey, you turn me on." Monk aped her behavior for a moment then stopped to help her unzip the costume. She pulled the mask off, laughing.

"I've always wanted to dress up in one of these," she admitted.

"We'll get some more and have a whole troupe of gorillas. Maybe we can do a dance number. J.S. offered to write some music the other night."

"Yeah, but who would play it? We can't afford a band, can we?"

Involved in the discussion, Monk took the gorilla mask off and scratched his head. At the same moment a small, smartly dressed woman of middle age marched around the corner of the house. When she saw Monk's head emerge from the costume, she stopped and gave a small shriek. Both Monk and Phoebe looked up.

The woman had short, perfectly styled dark hair with liberal threads of silver running through it, and her high-heeled shoes didn't even bring the top of her head up to Monk's collarbone. But that didn't stop her from poking an expensively gloved finger into his grubby sweatshirt.

"I suppose it's no more than I should expect," she said, her voice a little shrill. "Your brother told me what you were doing, but I would never have believed that a son of mine would make a monkey out of himself!"

Monk sighed and turned to Phoebe. "This is my mother," he said, his voice resigned. "Guinevere Malory Brown. Mom, this is Phoebe Sullivan, my landlady and fellow gorilla."

"Charmed," his mother snapped without looking at Phoebe. "Monk, pack your things. This has gone on long enough. I want you to come home with me."

8

THOUGH MONK HAD DISCARDED the tailcoat and deerstalker hat, he still wore the baggy sweatpants in which he practiced his routines. Tossing a juggling ball up and down one-handedly, he listened with a tightly drawn face to his mother's harangue.

Guinevere Brown paced up and down the living room, throwing her arms about with every phrase. "Can't imagine...ignominy! My own son...betrayal!"

Phoebe was in the kitchen, waiting for the water to boil for coffee. But she could hear Monk's mother, whose excitable voice had a piercing quality. Her heart went out to Monk, whose voice she hardly heard at all.

While the coffee dripped, Phoebe moved over to the back door to get out of earshot. Out in the yard Laura and Jim were handling the juggling clinic, teaching the principles of partner juggling. They whizzed the big Indian clubs back and forth with a nonchalance that amazed Phoebe.

Marlene and Bobby Newton were practicing side-by-side juggling, their young faces alight with interest. Looking at them, Phoebe had to smile. Their sibling fights had been celebrated in the neighborhood as spectacles of knockdown, drag-out technique. Now for the sake of Monk's troupe they could stand next to each other and trade juggling balls with rarely a break in the pattern they created.

She put the coffee on the tray and fussed with it, substituting her grandmother's delicate china for the mugs she usually used and adding the milk and sugar and silver teaspoons. There were cookies in the cookie jar, and she arranged some on a plate, cramming one into her mouth in response to the nervousness that plagued her. Monk wasn't likely to leave the boarding-house because his mother told him to. But the woman might be able to influence him to return to the corporation. Phoebe let her eyes linger on Monk as she carried the tray into the living room. She felt a cold darkness inside her when she thought of not seeing him every day.

"Thank you," Monk's mother said when Phoebe brought in the tray. "You may put it there." She pointed to the library table against the wall.

Phoebe blinked and set the tray down, but when she would have left the room, Monk grabbed her hand. "Please stay," he said, looking at her with a flash of vulnerability. She shook her head, but didn't pull away. She was curious about his mother, and she wanted to give him moral support if he needed it.

Mrs. Brown looked at her with a frown. "Merlin," she said impatiently, "you agreed to hear me out."

"Go ahead, Mom." Monk laced his fingers with Phoebe's. "I'm listening."

After another dissatisfied look at Phoebe, Monk's mother went back to her diatribe with renewed vigor.

"I hope I'm not one of those dictatorial parents who are always thinking they have their children's best interests at heart," she began, resuming her pacing and arm waving. "But the fact is, I do have your best interests at heart, my dear. What kind of retirement plan does this crazy scheme of yours offer? What kind of profit sharing? What fringe benefits? Do you see what you're doing to your future? You won't be thirty-five forever. Sooner or later you're going to need some security, and where will you get it?"

"The trust fund?" Monk's words were mild. Phoebe saw that his eyes had begun to twinkle.

"But that's not even enough to live on, let alone to put by for the future!" His mother stared at him, horrified. "What's more, a few bad investments on the trustees' part and the fund wouldn't even buy gasoline for that—that wreck you insist on driving!"

Monk chuckled. "Mom, the trust income seems adequate to me. And I've been banking a good portion of it every year. Right now I live on less than that."

"Less than—oh, poor baby." She stopped pacing and came over to put her hands along his cheeks. "You don't need to starve yourself, poor thing. Come along with me now, and I'll feed you up a little." She eyed his slim body with displeasure. "You're as thin as a rail."

Monk put her hands away from him gently. "I'm in good shape, Mom. I've got enough money for my needs, and I'm getting to start my own performing troupe—a chance to preserve comedic heritage and give people a good time, too. That's something few grown men have an opportunity to do." He turned away, toying idly with the books piled on the library table. "Why can't you understand and support me?"

"Well, of course I support you, sweetie. You're my baby." Monk's mother put her hand on his arm. "That's why I want only the best for you."

Again Monk swung away. "You just want me to juggle the company books instead of the things I want to juggle." His voice exasperated, he sent three paperbacks spinning through the air. His mother ducked as though the books were aimed at her, and Monk let them stop. "Listen, Mom. I'm going to do this. I love it, I won't quit it, and nothing you can say will stop me."

Mrs. Brown threw up her hands again. "The disgrace!" she proclaimed loudly. "Everyone knows that my family comes from the courtly tradition. You are a direct descendant of Sir Thomas Malory, but you choose to violate our family honor by acting like a fool!"

Phoebe bristled indignantly. "Just because Monk would rather play a jester than a knight in armor doesn't mean he's a fool!"

Monk bowed over her hand, kissing it gracefully and holding it to his heart. "My champion," he murmured.

Mrs. Brown squared off in front of Phoebe. "I don't know what business it is of yours, Mrs . . . uh, er, but this man has an illustrious family name and business to live up to. If you have designs on him—"

"This has gone far enough." Monk stepped between the two women and pushed his mother into a chair. "Just sit there for a minute and listen, if you can, Mom." He poured her a cup of coffee, added some milk and thrust the cup and saucer into her hands. Picking up a cookie, he approached her sternly.

"But Monk—"

Monk stuffed the cookie neatly into her mouth. "Now eat the cookie, so you won't try to interrupt me. Mom, I spent years in corporate finance before I realized I wanted to do something different before I die. This was not a spur of the moment decision for me. You simply chose to tune out all the evidence of my discontent."

Mrs. Brown chewed frantically and swallowed, but Monk handed her another cookie before she could start talking. "Now you're going to have to accept that my decision is made. There are plenty of people capable of doing what I did for ball bearings. There may be no one else capable of bringing Laughs Unlimited into being."

His mother groaned. "It gives me a spasm just to think about it." She grabbed his hand hopefully. "You will at least use an assumed name?"

He disengaged his hand and helped her to her feet. "Maybe I could switch from Brown to something less conspicuous.... Perhaps Smith?"

"That's good. Change your name. And Merlin... we'll be waiting when you come to your senses." She got to her feet and headed for the plate of cookies. "These are fabulous," she said, for the first time looking fully at Phoebe and smiling naturally.

"Thanks," Phoebe said hesitantly. "Oatmeal raisin chocolate chip."

"Marvelous." Mrs. Brown helped herself to another cookie. "No wonder you like this boardinghouse," she said to Monk.

Phoebe decided that maybe there was more to Mrs. Brown than met the eye. When she smiled, it was easy to see where Monk got his charm.

Monk saw his mother to the door and then came back to the living room, shaking his head. "She's losing it," he said gloomily. "Next thing you know she'll be wearing heraldic devices all over her clothes instead of just on the accessories."

"Does she really do that?" Phoebe took another cookie absentmindedly then caught Monk's eyes on her. She flushed and put the cookie back.

"Phoebe, love, you can eat as many cookies as you want. You don't have to deny yourself anything." Monk offered her the plate again, but she shook her head.

"I've been doing pretty well with denial lately—I mean as regards food," she added hastily.

Monk put the plate down. "And other things, too." He looked at her, his eyes blazing that bone-shaking crystal fire, and then they were in each other's arms, lips meeting hungrily, hands roaming feverishly. He tore his lips away to growl into her ear. "Any minute now some kid's going to come in here, or your mother will get home from her bird-watching, or *my* mother will come prancing back in. Phoebe, I'm dying in the midst of plenty here. When can we—"

"I don't know, Monk!" Phoebe pressed herself against him wantonly, afire in every part of her body. She had yearning aches in some powerful places, aches that had been growing since the previous Saturday's fiasco.

Not once in the week since they'd been together on Phoebe's bed had there been an opportunity for them to finish what they'd started. If they stayed up late in the living room, hoping to neck on the couch, Angie would stay up, too, or J.S. would get in early from his gig.

If they wandered upstairs to Monk's room, the children would come looking for new juggling challenges. If they canoodled in the porch swing, Phoebe's mother would just be getting back from some outing.

"The frustration is intense," Monk moaned in her ear, and Phoebe had to agree. She felt as if something was conspiring to keep them apart. So when the doorbell sounded, it was with a sense of resignation that Phoebe pulled away from Monk and went to answer it. Of course they would be interrupted again. Every time he'd taken her in his arms during the past week they'd been interrupted.

Standing outside the door was the florist, with whom she was on pretty good terms lately. He was holding the usual box of roses. Although she'd been thrilled to get them the first couple of times Tanner had sent them, somehow the thrill was gone now, and any container that was big enough to hold long-stemmed roses was already crammed full.

She signed for the flowers and brought them inside. Monk joined her in the hall, his face wearing the tight, noncommittal look that any reference to Tanner brought out. "This means another trip to the nursing home," Phoebe grumbled, taking the lid off the box and regarding the velvety blooms with a jaundiced eye. "Those old folks are going to get hay fever if this keeps up."

"You didn't open the card," Monk pointed out, his expression watchful.

Phoebe pulled the card out of its little envelope. "Only two more weeks, darling," she silently read Tanner's spiky script. "I'll be seeing you soon."

Two more weeks. She glanced down at herself, suddenly insecure. True, she'd had to buy new blue jeans, and all her shirts were fashionably baggy now. But her body was still nothing special, still generous as to hips and breasts, with none of the thinness that seemed to be the highly desired ideal in the Western world.

"He'll be here in two weeks." Phoebe's voice was hollow, and Monk gritted his teeth when he saw the uncertainty on her face. He wished Tanner were coming the next day, so they could get it over with, so Phoebe could make her choice. When the roses had begun arriving, he'd started to feel he and Tanner were in competition: Tanner would shower the lady with expensive gifts and his own famous presence; Monk would teach her to juggle and make her part of his troupe. Which one was Phoebe likely to prefer?

He wanted to pull her back into his arms where she belonged, but of course the phone rang before he could do that. Cursing under his breath, he gave up and went out to the jugglers in the backyard.

Phoebe watched him stride out the door, his neck held rigid. She could guess what caused the rigidity—

the same thing that had her tossing and turning at night in a bed that suddenly seemed much too large for one person.

Sherman Tofflerson of the Lindbergh Drug Store was on the phone. "I've had a chance to go over your copy," he said importantly. Sherman loved throwing advertising buzz words around to foster the impression that he knew all the ins and outs of it. "Can you come down?"

"Now?" She thought longingly of the partner juggling going on in the backyard; she had wanted to try her hand with the clubs. "It's Saturday."

"I won't have any time Monday, and the deadline to get the comps in is Tuesday, as you know."

Phoebe sighed. One of the hazards of self-employment was being at the beck and call of her clients. "I'll be right down."

She stopped to make sure someone would keep an eye on the little boys, changed into more respectable clothes and bicycled the six blocks to the drugstore. The weather was beautiful—so far not too hot and muggy. All around, trees were wearing their brightest green leaves, and bridal wreath bloomed in the yards of the old houses.

Sherman's drugstore was cool and dark inside. It was one of the old-fashioned stores, with a soda fountain in the back. Sherman presided from the prescription counter, perched on a high stool so he could see everything that went on. He interspersed his sales chat with exhortations to the soda jerk to snap it up.

"Only one scoop of ice cream in a float," he was shrieking as Phoebe walked up to him.

Two well-dressed ladies stood waiting for a prescription, one of them in a state of some agitation. She was taking a packet of tissues from her Gucci bag. "They just canceled," she told her companion unbelievingly. "Said they had a chance to be on TV in Chicago, so they wouldn't be able to do the benefit! Can you imagine?"

"Horrid for you, Gloria." The other lady groped in *her* Gucci bag and presented Sherman with one of an assortment of credit cards. "Entertainers can be so thoughtless."

"But what are we going to do?" Gloria wailed. "The benefit is in two weeks! Who can we find in that length of time?"

"I'm sure you'll find someone." The other woman put the charge card back. "You did want to chair the entertainment committee. As you'll recall, Mirium Levy was willing to do it again."

"She does it every year." Gloria sniffed and tucked the tissue back in her bag. "Maybe I can get one of the TV personalities, since it's such a worthy cause."

Phoebe was listening to their conversation absently when a light bulb flashed on in her head. Monk was looking for some kind of forum to launch Laughs Unlimited, and here was a community organization looking for benefit entertainment! It seemed predestined, somehow.

Gloria's friend picked up her prescription, and they were turning to leave when Phoebe, without taking time to think about it, planted herself in the way. "Excuse me, ma'am. I couldn't help but overhear your dilemma."

The two women swept Phoebe with comprehensive eyes that took in her lack of anything from Gucci. "Yes?" Gloria was not impolite, but she certainly didn't exude warmth.

"I think I can help you if you're looking for entertainment. I know this great European-style performing group—"

The word "European" caused the women to prick up their ears, and Phoebe hastily told them a little about Monk's troupe of jugglers, mimes and acrobats. While Sherman harassed the soda jerk about the proper way to make a milk shake, Phoebe and Gloria traded phone numbers. Their parting was much more cordial than their greeting had been.

Phoebe watched the door close behind them, listening to Sherman's strictures on her copy with only half her mind. The other half was seeing Laughs Unlimited opening the annual benefit for the prestigious Children's Health Association. She could hardly wait to tell Monk.

Doubts assailed her as she at last pedaled her bike home. Was two weeks too short a time for them to pull their act together? Would they be able to rent or make all the costumes they'd need?

She pushed the doubts firmly out of her mind. Monk had to get off the ground at the beginning of summer if he was going to have any sort of season at all. This opportunity would be tailor-made.

When she told him about it, over hastily prepared tuna sandwiches, Monk was so quiet she was afraid she'd overreached herself. "Monk?" She looked at him searchingly. "Is it a bad idea? I have her number; we can call and tell her to forget it."

"No way!" A broad grin split Monk's face. "I'm just...totally flabbergasted! I was worried about where we could perform, but I was scared to go out and find some place. And you just waltz into Sherman Toffler-son's and . . ." Words failed him, but he pulled Phoebe up with a half-eaten sandwich in her hand and waltzed her around the dining room, to the edification of the boys and Elizabeth.

Phoebe protested, laughing. "Now Monk, let's get sensible here! I'm getting tuna fish all over the rug! C'mon, now, let go, you animal!"

"Animal," Jamie repeated with satisfaction. "Monk's an animal! Monk's an old monkey face!"

His brother was only too pleased to join in the chant, and Phoebe was forced to send them off early for their afternoon naps. When she came back from washing the tuna off their hands and tucking them into bed, Monk was on the phone—with Gloria Taylor, the woman Phoebe had met in the drugstore. He grinned and gave her a thumbs-up, while nodding his head to the voice on the phone.

Elizabeth sat placidly at the table, finishing her sandwich and observing the commotion. Phoebe plopped down beside her. "Isn't this exciting?" She picked up a carrot stick and munched it for something to do until Monk was off the phone.

"I suppose." Elizabeth nodded, looking from Monk to her daughter and back again. "He's a nice fellow," she said abruptly. "What are you going to do about him?"

"Do? Why should I do anything?" Phoebe looked up in consternation.

"It's as plain as a pikestaff—the feeling that's between the two of you." Elizabeth held up her hand. "I'm not going to preach. Your life is your own, my dear, and you deserve happiness. Just be sure you know it when you see it. And don't trifle with someone's affections if you're not going to follow through."

Phoebe gulped. "Mom! As though I would.... I don't know, I guess I'm confused. There's Tanner...." She gestured toward the tall cut-glass vase overflowing with long-stemmed roses.

Her mother's face tightened. "That's just what I mean. You be careful, honey." She got up and carried her plate into the kitchen, passing Monk, who was still listening intently on the phone. Coming back through the dining room, she picked up her field glasses and gave Phoebe a meaningful look before heading out for her afternoon bird-watching expedition.

Phoebe propped her head in her hands and watched Monk while she mulled over her mother's unexpected outburst. Elizabeth rarely bothered with advice, feeling that everyone had to take charge of his or her own life. But when she did bother, it behooved the recipient to listen.

The trouble was, her mother's words didn't clarify anything. On the one hand, there was Tanner, courting by long-distance and expecting heaven only knew what from Phoebe when they finally got together. On the other hand, there was Monk, making himself indispensable in her house, in her life.

Strong emotions were seizing her, buffeting her in unfamiliar directions. She didn't know how to focus them. The sight of Monk practicing his slack-rope act in the backyard would give her helpless shivers of delight. But then, she'd gotten quite a thrill in the grocery store the other day when she'd spotted Tanner's face on the cover of *TV Guide*.

Monk hung up the phone at last and brought a big pad of paper over to the table. "So we've got it," he announced, a broad smile lighting his eyes. "Conditional on Gloria watching a rehearsal. I managed to put her off until Tuesday, so we have time to get our act together. Now, how should we open the show?"

They spent the afternoon outlining their debut, Phoebe absenting herself only long enough to throw together a giant casserole for dinner. The little boys got up and zoomed through the room on their way to rescue Rufus from incarceration in the backyard. The boarders drifted through, one after another; J.S. sat down at the battered piano in the living room and began to compose smooth, jazzy music to order, and Angie volunteered to get dressed up in spangled tights and hand out juggling implements.

"Good idea," Monk said briskly. He surveyed Edith, who had crept into the room in search of an apple from the fruit bowl on the sideboard. "We'll need you, too, Edith."

"I beg your pardon?" Edith dropped the apple and stared at Monk.

"You and Angie, to get dressed up in fancy costumes and help the crew. You'll hand out juggling equipment, move the slack rope around—I'll show you what to do." Observing Edith's terror-stricken paralysis, he added kindly, "You'll get paid, of course. Not much, but we've been guaranteed a percentage of the gate, and everyone will share in the take."

Phoebe glanced from Monk to Edith. She knew what he was trying to do. Edith had become more sociable since Monk's arrival, which was to say she could now exchange a whole sentence before scurrying back to her room. But it was a little abrupt to expect her to go from a brief conversation to dressing in spangles in front of a big audience.

She got up and started for the kitchen. "Edith, could you give me a hand with the vegetables?" Shutting the door, she led Edith to the kitchen table and handed her a carrot to scrape.

"Listen," she said, picking up a carrot of her own. "Monk is really up a creek right now. If he can't put together a good show by Tuesday, he may not be able to get his act off its feet at all this summer, and that probably means never."

Edith wasn't making much progress with her carrot. She raised frightened eyes to Phoebe and stuttered, "But why—why—"

"Why you? Because you're here, you're familiar with the act and he trusts you not to let him down." Phoebe pushed the carrots away and waited until Edith looked at her. "He needs us all to help him, and that means you too, Edith. He needs your help."

Edith bowed her head over her hands and sat for a minute. "I wouldn't have to say anything, would I?"

"Not a word, if you don't want to," Phoebe promised. "Monk can show you what needs to be done, and you can pick out the things you feel up to doing."

Taking a deep breath, Edith raised her head. "It terrifies me," she admitted frankly. "But I know I should do it. I *will* do it."

"Great." Phoebe hugged her then turned back to the carrot. "Now let's get this slaw finished. All this talking is making me hungry."

IT WAS LATE THAT NIGHT when Monk pushed the legal pad away from him and stretched. Everyone else except Phoebe was gone; the children and Elizabeth were in bed, Angie and J.S. were out, and Edith had vanished soon after dinner.

Phoebe was waiting up with him, feeling responsible for the flurry of activity and wanting to know how it turned out. She put down the book she'd been pretending to read and looked at Monk inquiringly.

"So this is the lineup for Laughs Unlimited."

Phoebe interrupted him. "Do you think that name's too obtuse for the folks around here?"

He shook his head decidedly. "No way. Everyone wants to be entertained, and real humor is such a rare gift."

"That's true."

"Now do you want to hear the lineup or not?" When she nodded meekly, he picked up a sheet of paper out of the welter that surrounded him. "Start off with a parade of jugglers, led by Laura and Jim. You'll be one of them."

"Me?" Phoebe stared at Monk in consternation. "I don't know how to juggle well enough for that."

"You'll do fine with a little more practice," Monk said absently. "The fancy stuff will be done by Laura and Jim. I'll come out and klutz around, get in the way, finally end up with five clubs in the air. Then the crew will set up the slack rope. Laura and Jim have a slack-rope routine, and they can do that. Then Cynthia O'Neill—she's a friend of Laura's—will do a tap dance number. Afterward we'll bring out the giant water balloon and let the audience toss it around a bit—that's always popular. Then Laura, Jim, Marlene and I will do your skit, and we'll wind up with everybody in gorilla costumes, marching around the stage. Do you think Jamie and Brendan would like to be chimps in the finale?"

"They'd expire with delight." Phoebe chewed her lower lip. "It sounds like lots of fun, but . . . Monk, we only have two gorilla costumes, and no one but you and Laura and Jim have those fancy tights."

"We'll rent from a costumer." Monk waved her objection aside. "I've been saving up my money for a long time, and I'm going to do it right. The better we look, the more bookings we'll get out of it."

"Who's going to handle the bookings?"

"Good question." Monk ran his hands through his hair, making it stick up in spikes. "There's lots of managerial work to be done, and I don't feel justified in hiring anyone to do it until we have some success." He looked at her helplessly. "If I paid you, would you help me with the paperwork?"

The question sent a frisson of unease through Phoebe. "I'll help you, of course," she said slowly. "But . . . I'm not sure I want to be paid."

Monk got to his feet and paced around on the faded carpet. "Of course you'll be paid." He crouched in front of Phoebe and took her hands in his warm clasp. "You can't afford to work for free, Phoebe, love. Charge me the same rate you charge for advertising clients." He forestalled the protest she wanted to utter by putting one hand lightly over her mouth. "Otherwise I won't be able to take up your time."

"All right," she said finally. "I'll keep a record of the time I spend for you and submit a bill after the performance." She could fudge the record so it reflected fewer hours. Every dollar that Monk had saved for the troupe was precious, and it wasn't fair that he should pay the same hourly rate for simple paperwork that her clients did for full creative firepower.

But even though the money involved wouldn't be much, the knowledge that Monk would pay her at all made her feel constrained around him. Suddenly things seemed different between them. Before they had been cohorts in bringing a dream to life; now business had reared its ugly head.

"Well," she said uncertainly, getting to her feet. "Guess I'll go to bed." *Before the house starts burning down, or a burglar breaks in, or some other horrible thing happens to keep us from being alone together,* she thought.

"Phoebe..." Monk put a hand on her arm and pulled her around to face him. "This doesn't change anything between us," he whispered urgently. "You know how I feel about you."

"Well..." That was the trouble, Phoebe thought hazily, trying to keep her lips from fastening of their own volition on Monk's. She knew they shared an extremely potent sexual desire. But he'd never again mentioned love, and she'd never got up the nerve to ask him about it. So she didn't really know how he felt. She didn't really know how she felt. She only knew that this man was important in her life. No one else she'd known since Danny could make her feel so weak, so wanted.

She raised her eyes to his, hoping that he would read in them what she was unable to ask for with words. "Phoebe," Monk said hoarsely, "I was going to wait until after Tanner—oh my God, Tanner!"

"What? Huh?" Phoebe tried to clear her thoughts. They had been on the verge of kissing, and this time they might actually have made it to her bedroom without interruption. And then Monk had brought up Tanner. "I swear, sometimes I think you don't really want to make love with me," she said crossly. "Why the hell did you have to drag Tanner in tonight, of all nights?"

Monk dropped her arms and stepped back, his face grave. "Tanner will be here in two weeks. You told me so yourself." She stared blankly at him, and he frowned in impatience. "Our benefit is in two weeks! Don't you see, you've got a conflict, Phoebe! What are you going to do?"

Phoebe closed her eyes in dismay. She had a conflict, all right—a classic one—and she didn't know how to resolve it.

"Let me know what you decide," Monk said stiffly, moving to the door. "I could replace you in the skits." Before she could reply, he was heading up the stairs to his room.

She stared at his retreating back, her hands on her hips. "Oh, could you?" Muttering, she locked up the house and flounced into her own bedroom. "Well, thanks for nothing!" She would stick by Monk, of course. There was no doubt about that.

But he had made a big mistake. If he hadn't been so stiff-necked about it, she could have seized on the performance as a good excuse to get out of her date with Tanner. Instead, Monk had got into a snit.

His attitude had insured one thing: she would find a way to see Tanner as well as fulfill her duties to the troupe.

9

THE BACKYARD was a seething swirl of would-be performers and excited neighbors, both adults and children. Phoebe defended the huge box of gorilla costumes from determined assaults by every kid who lived on the block. "Why did school have to let out today?" she moaned to Edith, who helped her drag the box behind the garage, where a backstage dressing area had been improvised. "These kids don't seem to understand that we're not doing this strictly for their benefit."

Edith nodded, rubbing a spot of dirt off the shiny fabric of her short full-skirted gold lamé dress. With tights to match and makeup applied by Angie's lavish hand, she had been transformed. Her mousy hair was hidden under a glittery bowler hat, and her smile flashed out often. But the biggest transformation came from her newly liberated eyes. She had gone out and had herself fitted for contact lenses. Without the heavy glasses, her eyebrows no longer seemed to meet in the center of her face.

"You look great," Phoebe told her impulsively. "It's fun to play dress up, isn't it?"

Edith nodded again. "I feel like a different person," she said in a rush then frowned. "That's a dreadful cliché, but it's true. It's like it isn't *me* in here, so it doesn't matter if I. . . well, shake my booty." To Phoebe's surprise, Edith did just that, looking saucily over her shoulder as she whisked around the corner.

"Right *on,*" Phoebe muttered. She skirted the chaos of the backyard and went around to check the front.

Elizabeth had been stationed on the porch to guide Gloria Taylor into the performance area after warning the waiting troupe so they could properly dispose themselves. She looked up from the bird guide she studied as Phoebe came onto the porch. "How's it going back there?" Closing the book, she squinted up at her daughter. "The noise is enough to wake the dead. . . and what a great costume!"

"Isn't it?" Phoebe preened herself a little. Monk had chosen costumes with a lavish hand. Angie, who was currently in charge of makeup behind the garage, had bagged a skintight latex unitard in gleaming stripes of purple and gold, highlighted with a saucy little skirt and topped by a hat identical to Edith's. Phoebe loved her own costume best, though. All the jugglers were dressed alike in trousers gathered at the ankle, topped by full-sleeved tunics. The fabric was patterned with red, blue and green diamonds, and they wore small red satin caps on their heads. "They're designed after traditional Harlequin costumes, as a nod at the commedia del l'arte style."

"Did Monk buy them?" Elizabeth rubbed a fold of the fabric between her fingers. "The material's kind of sleazy, don't you think?"

"He rented them for the day," Phoebe explained, "with option to extend the rental period for a month if Mrs. Taylor wants us to do the show. He might buy them. I don't know." She stroked the gleaming satin of her tunic. "It feels great to wear. I don't think it's sleazy at all."

Elizabeth shook her head and opened the bird book again. "Waste of money, if you ask me," she sniffed. "We could have made costumes better than that."

"Maybe you should put in a bid if we get to do the benefit." Phoebe made the suggestion half jokingly, but her mother looked up with interest.

"That's an idea. Maybe I will. If that young man is going to throw his money around, he might as well throw some my way."

Two cars pulled up to the curb, and Gloria Taylor got out of one of them. "Stall them for a few minutes," Phoebe murmured before escaping through the house.

Monk had managed to quell the chaos in the backyard by the simple expedient of beginning the juggling. The neighbors had settled on the scuffed lawn around the edges of the practice ring. Children and adults watched enraptured as he juggled items tossed to him from the audience—a wristwatch, a coffee cup, a sneaker, a wallet and a pocket diary. "Can I keep what's in the wallet?" he called. His audience laughed, and Marlene's dad, who evidently owned the wallet, called back, "You can keep anything you can get out of it while juggling."

Phoebe hated to break it up, especially since Monk seemed to be succeeding at extracting a dollar bill from the wallet while he juggled it along with four other unrelated objects. But it was time to show Gloria Taylor their stuff.

"She's here!" At her words the audience looked up alertly, and Monk began to toss the items he was juggling back to their owners.

"I'm glad you've all come to watch our tryout today," he told the crowd. "Please feel free to laugh, hiss, boo and otherwise enjoy yourself. But please also respect the performers, and don't get in our way. And if you could keep an eye on your little ones, that would be very helpful."

Phoebe remembered that she still had the gorilla costumes to hang out, and she rushed to join the rest of the troupe waiting behind the garage. As she hefted the furry outfits, Ross Belden stopped flirting with Angie and came to help. He had agreed to be on the crew, and that was useful since he was expert at manipulating the heavy slack-rope apparatus. But it had taken a lot of effort to get him to change his usual sweat suit for one of the sleek unitards Monk wanted everyone to wear. "*I* feel like the monkey around here," he complained as he picked up one of the gorilla masks. "Does my ol' pal expect me to cram myself into one of these things, too?"

"Not unless you want to." Phoebe shook out the last costume and hung it on the clothesline that had been strung along the back of the garage.

Monk was giving the troupe a pep talk. "Someday," he said, his gaze traveling proudly over the eager performers, "we'll have our own tent, with a place for the band and everything." As if to underscore his words,

J.S. and a couple of buddies he'd recruited struck up a tune from their makeshift bandstand at the side of the garage. Piano, saxophone and drums blended in J.S.'s bouncy jazzy conception of circus music and sent tingles of excitement through Phoebe. This was it! In the next couple of hours the future of Laughs Unlimited would be determined.

She peeked around the corner of the garage, checking out the slack rope that was set up at the back of the performance space, the huge water balloon that quivered at the edge of the garage, the wooden platform for the tap dance number. Behind her the neat ranks of costume changes swayed in the breeze.

When she looked out again, her mother was guiding Gloria Taylor and another woman to their VIP chairs on the back porch. She felt Monk's warm breath on her neck as he came up close behind her. "Give me a squeeze for luck," he whispered, and Phoebe turned gladly to comply. Their relationship had been submerged in the frantic activity of the past few days. There had been no time for physical closeness, and Phoebe had missed it. She gave herself up to Monk's hasty embrace.

Then he looked over her head at the back porch and groaned. "Oh, no!"

Phoebe craned her neck. "What's the matter?" Everything looked in order to her: the audience of neighbors, their faces alight with anticipation; the elegant Gloria Taylor, smiling and chatting to the woman who sat beside her.

"Elaine," Monk muttered, pushing Phoebe away. "That's torn it."

Just then the music picked up as J.S., seeing that the guest of honor was seated, began the parade theme, and everyone lined up to march into the yard.

The first few minutes were a blur to Phoebe, and she completely forgot Monk's consternation at the sight of Elaine, whoever she might be. He seemed to have forgotten it, too.

The troupe was in fine fettle. They had spent the past two days practicing, so everyone knew what to do. Their appearance as they pranced around the yard, throwing brightly colored confetti into the audience, provoked spontaneous cheers. Laura and Jim, in their spangled leotards, led the parade, and the rest of the troupe followed. Last of all came Monk, wearing his shabby tailcoat and battered top hat, a big red nose, a red-and-white-striped T-shirt and indescribable shoes.

When it was time to begin juggling, Phoebe concentrated on what she was doing, but she couldn't keep a wide smile from pasting itself across her face. Monk was in top form, soliciting things from the audience again: a coffee cup, a baseball cap, an apple. He caught each item as it came up and added it to the collection he had whirling through the air, always seeming on the verge of dropping something and never quite doing so.

It seemed to Phoebe that the minutes swirled past as quickly as the balls she juggled. Everyone made mistakes, of course; she made her share. But momentary slipups couldn't dim the rush of excitement that was almost palpable in the ring.

Individual moments stood out: the water balloon bursting to shower the children in front with sparkling, iridescent drops of water, while Angie let a bunch of helium balloons soar into the high blue sky; Laura, poised on Jim's shoulders, launching herself into a perfect forward somersault and landing as gracefully as a butterfly on the bright yellow mat; Cynthia O'Neill's rapid-fire tapping to tunes from *A Chorus Line*.

Through it all J.S. wove magical music. Though the show moved at a fast clip, Phoebe felt a dreamlike, slow-motion quality to time. *I will never forget this,* she thought, standing in the background during the slack-rope act. She wanted to keep one little segment of time forever, one burnished gem, to have with her for the rest of her life.

But time wouldn't oblige and hustled on regardless. J.S. gave the music cue for the final skit. Phoebe slipped around to beckon to her sons and, forewarned, they tiptoed from the audience with noisy care to join her.

Behind the garage a transformation was going on. Silky leotards disappeared into hairy bodies. Jamie and Brendan stood openmouthed as Jim, his gorilla head firmly in place, jumped up and down, scratching and making ape noises. He took the head of the costume off to show them it was really he, and their momentary uncertainty turned to delight.

Onstage Monk began the skit, using his oversize magnifying glass, stalking to and fro in his indescribable shoes. Phoebe climbed into her own costume after suiting the little boys up as chimps. They looked adorable, and before she put the head of her costume on, she stored a picture of them in her mental scrapbook.

They waited behind the garage for their cue, and then they were out, tumbling and chasing in what was supposed to be well-choreographed disarray. But the little boys were too excited to remember exactly what they were supposed to do, and their antics made chaos out of the practiced scene.

At last Phoebe took their hairy paws in hers and began to dance with them. Everybody started dancing—steps that were suspiciously like the aerobic dances Monk did at the gym. They looked fine, though, when performed by a crowd of gorillas and a couple of disheveled detectives.

The climax was over. Ross sent the last of the balloons soaring, the gorillas tossed the last of the confetti, and the band belted out the last few bars of music while the troupe danced off behind the garage.

There were tears in Phoebe's eyes as she slipped out of the heavy fur. It had been an incredible experience. Even if Laughs Unlimited didn't get to do the Children's Health Association benefit, she had at least got to take part in Monk's dream. Her tears were for the excitement, the inevitable letdown, the joy of having done it, the sadness that it was over.

Monk came over to her. He'd stripped off his baggy costume and red nose. In his leotard, with his hair tousled from the deerstalker hat, he looked incredibly sexy to her. She couldn't understand why every woman in the audience wasn't trying to mob him.

"I've got to talk to Mrs. Taylor before Elaine screws everything up," he said urgently. "Could you go out and get her away? Take her into the house, knock her over the head—just do something with her."

"With whom? Elaine?" Phoebe hurried after him as he cut through the elated throng of performers and neighbors, who were beginning to mingle. She took a moment to entrust the expensive gorilla costumes to Ross then put on a burst of speed until she caught up with Monk again.

Mrs. Taylor was talking to him, all smiles and graciousness. The woman Phoebe had taken to be her companion was standing back a little, tapping one foot impatiently. Glancing from her to Monk, Phoebe understood. Elaine was undoubtedly another member of the courtly Malory Brown family. She had the same thick brown hair as Monk, only hers had been blown-dry to a glossy finish. She was nearly as tall as Monk and beautifully dressed, with diamonds flashing in her earlobes and on her fingers.

Phoebe swallowed, wondering how she was expected to hustle a woman who radiated such self-assurance. However, Monk had asked her to do it. So she went up with her best smile on. "How do you do? You're Monk's sister, aren't you? He asked me to take you into the house and make you comfortable while he finishes his business."

Elaine looked Phoebe up and down, and a slow smile dawned on her face. "You must be Monk's landlady," she said in a deep, pleasant voice. "Mama said you were attractive." She took Phoebe's arm. "Lead the way, landlady. Do you have any more of those cookies?"

Bemused, Phoebe allowed herself to be escorted into her own kitchen. Waiting for the water to boil, they sat at the table and munched on cookies from Phoebe's bottomless jar.

Elaine was full of questions about the performance. How long had it taken to put together the troupe? Was Monk paying everyone? Was it true that they were going to headline the benefit for the Children's Health Association?

"If it is true, Mama will just go nuts," Elaine said cheerfully, accepting a cup of jasmine tea. "She's prominent in that organization, you know, and she's convinced Monk's going to bring disgrace on us all."

"Nonsense." Phoebe plunked her own cup down. "There's no disgrace in working hard at something you love like Monk loves performing."

"And you?" Elaine chuckled. "No, you needn't bother answering. It's plain to see. Even Mama noticed, and she can't see much of what's beyond her nose." She crunched another cookie and patted Phoebe's hand consolingly. "Don't worry. Mama and Lance may fuss, but they won't stand in Monk's way. He's the baby, so he'll get what he wants."

"Does that bother you?" Elaine's friendly manner had set Phoebe enough at ease to let her blurt out a personal question. She started to retract it, but Elaine paid no attention.

"It used to." Monk's sister stared into her teacup. "I was the middle one, and his arrival put my nose out of joint. But I was reconciled when I realized I could boss him around." She laughed. "It's been years now since he politely but firmly told me to mind my own business. But the temptation to boss him is still strong. I have given him my unsolicited advice pretty often in the past." She looked up at Phoebe, her eyes twinkling. "Is that why he sent you to separate me from Gloria? I bet it was. I bet he was afraid I was going to start telling him what to do in front of her."

"I don't know about that." Phoebe refilled the cups and tried to look oblivious despite Elaine's knowing expression.

"It really is none of my business." Elaine looked at the cookie plate and pushed it away with a groan. "I just came by out of sheer vulgar curiosity. Mama was a little incoherent, and I wanted to see for myself what Monk was up to. Gloria and I arrived together by pure chance. She probably thought I was trying to muscle in on her committee."

"Are you part of the CHA, too?"

"I belong." Elaine shrugged. "I send a donation every year and serve on the board when I can't get out of it." She looked at Phoebe ruefully. "When you have means, the local charities are constantly at you for money and volunteer time. What with work and my family, I don't have much spare time."

"I can understand that, I suppose," Phoebe murmured. "Where do you work?"

"Didn't Monk tell you?" Elaine's eyebrows climbed her forehead. "For the illustrious company, of course. Brown Bearings. I'm head of marketing." She stood up and stretched before she carried her cup over to the sink. "Monk is the only one to have escaped the golden yoke. That's why Lance is so prissy about it. Really, he envies Monk his freedom. As do I, of course."

"Bull, Sis." Monk stood in the back door, relaxed and looking superb, the late afternoon sun gilding the firm musculature beneath his leotard. "You don't envy me. You like your fancy office and the perks and the salary."

Elaine gave Monk a big hug and held him off to look at him. "You look fabulous, Monkey-man. I was just telling Phoebe here how much in awe of your abilities I am. The performance was terrific."

Monk returned his sister's hug then went to stand beside Phoebe, draping one arm loosely around her shoulders. For Phoebe's deprived sensory system, his touch set off clamorous yearnings. She only managed to keep herself from pushing him to the floor and kissing him senseless by exerting more control than she realized she had.

"Thanks," Monk was saying easily, "but I didn't do it alone. Some wonderful people have been putting in a lot of time to make this happen."

"Did Gloria want you for the benefit?" Phoebe couldn't wait any longer to know.

"Yes, she did." Monk's face split in a brilliant grin, and Phoebe gave him a delighted hug. "We're to headline. The benefit is actually going to take place in an outdoor tent, so even the ambience will be right. The financial arrangements are satisfactory, and she's already set up two talk-show dates for next week, for me to promote the troupe."

"Great!" Elaine pumped Monk's hand. "You'll have a big audience. I know they sold out last year, and they're expecting to again this year." She gave Monk an impish smile. "I think Brown Bearings will probably buy a big block of tickets, since it's for a good cause."

Monk laughed. "It's good to know that you didn't come to chew me out, Elaine. I've had everyone but the Big Guy himself on my neck already." A look of alarm crossed his face. "Good grief, he's not coming, is he?"

Elaine shook her head, her smile fading a little. "He's up to his ears with that acquisition Lance told you about. But he asked me to tell you he knows you have a good head on your shoulders, and what you do with it is your choice." She picked up her handbag from the table. "Maybe we can persuade him to show up for your benefit."

"I hope so." Monk drew Phoebe with him as he walked Elaine to the door. "I'd like to see the old war horse before he works himself to death."

Phoebe didn't miss the edge of bitterness in his voice. After Elaine had gone, she watched Monk wander aimlessly around the living room, touching the books, the antimacassars, but not settling anywhere.

"Thinking about your father?"

He shot her a startled look. "As a matter of fact, yes. How did you guess?" Without waiting for an answer, he prowled over to the dining room archway and stood there, his head cocked toward the backyard. "They're still going strong out there," he remarked with a slight smile. Phoebe could hear the sounds of J.S.'s piano above the steady hum of many voices. "It's like a block party."

"Uhmm." Chewing her lip, Phoebe gazed blindly at the bookcase, where the sun lingered on the faded gilt spines of the Cherry Girls adventure books her grandmother had collected as a girl. "Y'know, my father died just after I got pregnant with Jamie. He'd been hassling me for years to give him a grandchild to spoil, and I had laughed it off like there was plenty of time. I've always felt a little guilty that we didn't get around to having children sooner."

"It wouldn't matter to my dad." Monk shrugged irritably and resumed his restless prowling. "Lance and Elaine each had the requisite number of kids after obtaining the requisitely proper spouse. They all have dinner together every Sunday. Afterward, my dad throws the kids a twenty and tells them to study hard."

"Is that how it was when you were growing up?"

"We only got five." Monk smiled wryly. "There has been inflation, you know."

"Poor little rich boy," Phoebe murmured. The thought of anyone as warm and affectionate as Monk growing up in the cold sterile atmosphere of wealth was incongruous.

"Are you picturing me as a neglected rich kid?" He peered into her face, and sitting down next to her, he draped her shoulders again with his arm. "Nothing could be further from the truth. We lived in a big old house in Clayton, with lots of woods and wildlife around. I kept rabbits behind the garage. Lance and I careered around the neighborhood on our bikes—we had lots of friends nearby. Ross was one of them. My mother loved us all, and spent as much time with us as we'd let her, but we preferred the freedom to have adventures with the gang."

He sighed deeply. "I didn't really care then that my father was too busy working to do anything with us. But later when I began working, too . . ." He was silent for a minute, and Phoebe, her mind busy with the images he'd shared of his childhood, was not inclined to interrupt.

"Maybe," he said finally, "the reason why I hated being tied down at my job was that I feared turning into a man like my father. I couldn't see letting that kind of work be the most important thing in my life."

"I can understand that," she said softly. "I know the money would be steadier if I got a clerical job somewhere. But I burned out on that six months after graduating from college. The only job I could get was as a clerk-typist. The other people in the office were great, but I found out that I couldn't stand taking orders from the execs about things I felt I knew better than they did. I just don't want to work in those conditions again."

"Looks like we're both mavericks," Monk said with his endearing crooked smile. "Maybe we belong together."

She met his eyes, startled, her heart accelerating at the emotion in his voice. He had never before said anything that smacked of commitment. She knew because she'd been hovering on the brink of blurting out her own growing feelings for him many times.

She opened her mouth, but he put one finger over her lips. "Don't say anything now," he told her huskily. "I wasn't going to say anything, either, until after your buddy Tanner got here. I don't want to limit your choices, Phoebe, but I couldn't help letting you know how much you've come to mean to me."

Head spinning, Phoebe tried to take in what he was saying. "Monk," she whispered around the finger on her lips, "I don't . . . are we talking about the big L-O-V-E?"

He laughed shakily and gathered her close. "I'm not saying another word until . . . Wait a minute!" Jumping up, he dragged her to her feet and towed her across the floor to the kitchen. There he flipped the page on the calendar from May to June. On the Saturday of the benefit, the day after Phoebe's scheduled date with Tanner, he wrote in big letters, "Monk. Dinner, 7:00 P.M."

"There," he said, tossing the pen back into the pottery jar by the calendar and regarding his handiwork with satisfaction. "Go ahead and have your date with Mister TV. I really want you to do that. Then on Saturday, after the benefit, we'll go out, just the two of us. I'll be asking you a very important question then, Phoebe. A question having to do with juggling."

She looked up at him, puzzled. "Juggling? Monk, are we having the conversation I thought we were having?"

Smiling, he pulled her against him. "Of course, love. I was referring to partner juggling."

"Of course. Partner juggling. Now I understand everything." She nodded wisely, feeling an effervescence spring to life within her. Monk loved her. He must love her.

"You will," he muttered and covered her lips fiercely with his own. His touch brought the simmering fever instantaneously to a boil. A rolling boil, Phoebe thought incoherently, tasting his tongue delicately with her own. She could feel the passion roiling within her, spreading to every part of her body. Her breasts hardened against his chest, and her pelvis urgently sought to merge with his. The heat was unbearable. There would be an explosion...everything would boil over....

Gasping, Monk tore his lips away from hers, and she hung limply against him, her own chest heaving as she tried to regain control over her breathing. Only then did she notice their interested audience. Framed in the back door were Jamie and Brendan, and Elizabeth was behind them with Angie and J.S. craning their heads over Elizabeth's shoulder. Edith, very crimson of face, lurked behind everyone else.

Smiling weakly, Phoebe pulled away from Monk. "So," she said, fanning her heated face, trying to smile brightly, "is the party over?"

The little boys tumbled into the room, and the boarders followed. "I don't know," J.S. said, his gaze inquisitive. "You tell me. Looked like it was just gettin' started."

Phoebe turned her back on all of them and buried herself in the refrigerator. "Dinner time." Knowing from experience the fastest way to clear the kitchen, she said, "Who wants to help me fix it?"

In a few minutes only the boys were left in the room, with Monk lounging in the doorway.

"That won't be the end of it, you know," he said, watching her set out the ingredients for noodle dough.

"We explain nothing." Phoebe washed her hands grimly. She mounded flour on her pastry board, tossed eggs and water into a crater in the center of it and began mixing with her fingers. The little boys watched solemnly before Jamie ran to bring out the hand-crank pasta machine.

"That won't stop Angie. Oh, well," Monk said philosophically, moving into the kitchen, "I've gotten used to interruptions in my courting lately. It can't last forever."

A blush crept over her cheeks at the significant note in his voice. Her hands trembling, she didn't notice that she'd reversed directions in cranking the pasta dough, until Jamie yelled.

"Watch out, Mom!" Noodles were Jamie's favorite food, and he didn't intend to let them be sacrificed to his mother's absentmindedness. "Here, let me do it."

Phoebe relinquished control. She got salad ingredients out of the refrigerator and sat down by Monk at the table. He promptly put his arm around her. "Our cover's blown," he reminded her when she glanced worriedly at her sons. "We might as well get some good out of it."

"Let me get this straight." She searched his face, noting the tender expression in his eyes. "From now until my date with Tanner, we can—uh—"

"Make free with each other?" Monk's voice was hopeful. "Spend every minute in your bed? Get a great big jar of honey and—"

"Monk!" Phoebe looked at Brendan, who was watching them wide-eyed. "Please remember the young ears." She rapped Monk smartly on the knuckles with a piece of cucumber. "I got the impression from what you said that we were to be . . . well, pure or something until after Tanner's visit. No reason to on my account, of course," she added hastily. "I mean, we could just get that jar of honey—"

"Phoebe, love," Monk interrupted. "Your son is going to be carrying some very strange tales around." He squeezed her hand and got up again. "I meant every word I said and a lot more that I didn't. Now, if you'll excuse me, I need to take care of my equipment before dinner."

Seeing that he was going to leave, Phoebe abandoned all pretense at making salad. "Monk! I need to know—what are the rules here? You're the one who started this whole 'wait for Tanner' junk. It's not my idea, let me tell you!"

"I know, love." His smile was tender and disturbing, making it hard for her to concentrate on his words instead of the shape and texture of the lips saying them. "I can't promise not to kiss you into a stupor between now and then. But I can promise that nothing else will happen. Nothing at all."

10

ON THE EVENING of her date with Tanner, Phoebe came out of her bedroom to find the hall crowded.

Angie hovered anxiously, having been rebuffed in her offer to do Phoebe's makeup. Elizabeth stood in the living room archway just behind the boys, who gazed with awe at Phoebe's unaccustomed magnificence. J.S. lounged on the steps, dressed in his own evening finery, observing the commotion as though it was a show put on for his amusement. Even Edith, who had been helping Elizabeth with last minute trimming of costumes for the benefit the next day, stood by the steps, twisting her hands together and looking as if she wanted to bolt to her room.

Only Monk was missing. But Phoebe would be hanged if she'd ask where he was. She was doing this mainly because, for some unfathomable reason, Monk wanted her to. After the argument they'd had that afternoon, it was no wonder he wasn't there to see her carry out his wishes.

The quarrel had probably been due to the stress of getting ready for the benefit. Everyone in the house had felt pressured, since everyone had a stake in the survival of Laughs Unlimited. Elizabeth had gone around swathed in costume materials, even giving up her bird-watching excursions for the cause. She'd pressed Edith into helping her, and as the work mounted, Edith had blossomed. She'd even gone so far as to snap at Angie one night at dinner when Angie complained about the lack of décolletage in her costume.

Angie had spent some time with Monk, learning what he knew of makeup for mimes and clowns. She talked importantly of her role as a lovely helper and generally got on everyone's nerves. But she was an asset to the troupe, and Phoebe hadn't minded her rather transparent flirtation with Monk. Flirting with any man around was Angie's way.

J.S. had even gone so far as to get up before ten o'clock every morning to rehearse with the troupe. He claimed to be looking forward to the performance as the time of his release from such a barbaric practice, but Phoebe had noticed him turning up alertly that morning even though Monk had told everyone to take the day off.

And that had been a pity. Forced into inactivity by his decree, her combined nervousness over the night ahead of her and the performance the next day making her peevish, Phoebe had quarreled with Monk.

It had begun innocently enough. She had been in the kitchen, filling up the day by filling up the freezer. On the back of the stove chickens simmered in her big stockpot. Tomato sauce bubbled lazily in the second biggest pot. She was assembling two huge pans of lasagna, one for dinner that night and one for the freezer, when Monk had sauntered in and stopped with a frown.

"Why are you slaving over a hot stove when you should be resting up, woman?"

She looked at him, surprised. "I'm not slaving. I've been too busy to cook lately, and it seemed like a good opportunity."

"Just don't tire yourself out." Monk was still frowning. "You probably won't get much rest tonight, and you'll need to be fresh tomorrow."

"Now just what do you mean by that crack?" Phoebe put her hands on her hips and glared at him. "Not get much rest tonight, indeed. If you think I'm going to exhaust myself by hopping in the sack with Tanner Hayden, you couldn't be more wrong."

"Who knows what will happen?" White dents appeared on either side of Monk's nose, and his face tightened irritably. Fascinated, Phoebe realized that he was angry. More angry than she'd ever seen him.

"Monk—"

He was too angry to listen, that was for sure. "I heard you talking to him when he called night before last. The man has a line that doesn't quit!"

"Monk!"

"An intimate dinner, as they say in the romances. Soft lights. Tanner starts feeding you a line of bull about how he's never forgotten the incredible experience of being your lover. How he wants to take you back with him to Neverland and shower you with the good things in life. Before you know it, you're in his palatial hotel room and being impressed with champagne and all the trimmings. He pleads for you to take pity on him, surrounded as he is by all those mindless bimbos. He sobs that his life is empty, that he needs a good woman to—"

"Monk, for heaven's sake." Phoebe blinked and shook her head, clearing away the dramatic picture Monk had painted. "You were the one who kept telling me I had to do this. If it hadn't been for you, I would have told Tanner to forget it."

Monk rubbed a hand over his face, and she noticed the exhaustion around his eyes. For weeks he'd been tireless, seeing to details, anticipating needs, getting everything ready. And the emotional tension between the two of them couldn't have been exactly relaxing. She thought of the sleepless nights *she'd* spent.

Nevertheless, if it was making them both so miserable, why were they going through with the charade? "You know how we feel about each other, Monk. You won't talk about it, but we both know. Why were you so insistent that I do this?"

He turned to her and threw his arms out. "Why? If it comes to that, why didn't you just tell him to forget it on your own? You're an independent woman. You don't need me to tell you who to see and who not to see!"

Phoebe could get angry, too. "That's right, I don't! And I think I'll very much enjoy seeing Tanner again tonight."

He stared at her, his eyes the cold wintry blue of a frozen lake, and walked out of the room.

Phoebe wanted to call him back, to tell him that she loved him. But there was something in her that wanted a big TV star's stamp of approval to complete her fragile new self-confidence. Something that was proud of being sought by a national sex symbol.

So she had spent the afternoon getting ready for a date that could have far-ranging consequences. Although she doubted that Monk's scenario would come true, at least experiencing that kind of sumptuous seduction would be . . . interesting. Of course, she would ultimately say no to Tanner, whatever he requested.

She had bathed in the scented oil she had rescued from oblivion at the bottom of the bathroom cupboard. Taking a lot of time to do it, she had managed to blow-dry her hair into artless wisps that curled around her face. She had dug up eye makeup and used it to good effect.

The dinner gong went off while she was standing in her underwear in front of the wardrobe. Angie had wanted her to buy a new dress for this important date, but Phoebe had hooted at the idea that she spend her meager cash in such a fashion. Now she wished she'd listened. Most of her clothes were too big for her twenty pounds slimmer and infinitely trimmer body, and those that weren't were five years out of date.

At last she chose an antique embroidered silk blouse she'd found in a thrift shop once, and a wine-colored brocade skirt her mother had made for her in more flamboyant days. The skirt was narrow and fastened on the side, falling to midcalf length. The black slippers that were part of her juggling costume went well with the ensemble. She had crammed some money and a hanky into the mesh evening bag that had been her mother's and then had opened her door to find everyone assembled there, waiting.

Everyone but Monk.

It doesn't bother me that he wants to sulk, Phoebe told herself. He'd picked the fight with her, so he should be the one to apologize. How was she supposed to have known that he wanted her to break her date with Tanner? And why should she, when it had been made before she'd realized that she felt something special for Monk?

The justifications had a hollow ring, and she scanned the faces once more before realizing that Monk really meant to let her go to Tanner without trying to make his peace.

"You look lovely, dear," her mother said, smiling with pleasure at Phoebe. "That skirt always looked nice on you."

"It did before I had children, anyway." The words reminded her of her successful weight loss, which reminded her of Monk.

"Don't you think just the smallest bit of blush? No? Well, I guess you don't really need it." Angie brandished the small makeup case she held. "You look quite nice." She couldn't quite keep the surprise out of her voice.

"Stunning, m'dear," J.S. drawled. "A regular vision. Glamorous as all get out."

Angie wasn't allowing that. "Nonsense, J.S. Phoebe looks as nice as I've ever seen her, but glamorous? That outfit is too sedate for glamorous."

J.S. shrugged, and his satin lapels gleamed. "On you, yes. On Phoebe, no."

Angie sniffed. Any retort she might have made was lost in the peal of the doorbell.

The group in the hall looked at one another, and Phoebe felt her palms grow damp. Wiping them hastily on her skirt, she opened the door.

Tanner looked just as he had on the cover of *TV Guide*: his hair was gleaming, his eyes were brilliant, and his head was cocked to one side. He was instantly familiar, and yet a total stranger. Phoebe stared at him, wide-eyed.

He smiled lazily and held out another bunch of the ubiquitous red roses. "Bee, my dear," he murmured richly. "You are as fresh, as unchanged, as ever." He put the roses in her numb hands and gathered her up for a ritual hug, a kiss on both cheeks.

Hands still on her shoulders, he held her off for a quick survey. "This elegance—where is the madcap girl in frayed blue jeans?"

That brought Phoebe out of her fog. "If you wanted to see her, you should have gotten here a few hours ago."

He laughed and pushed her back inside. "Put your flowers in water," he said, following her into the house, "and we'll—"

Phoebe glanced back and saw that the earnest regard of six pairs of eyes had stopped him in his tracks. "Let me introduce you to everyone, Tanner," she said, hoping that Angie wouldn't embarrass her. "Angie Molinaro, bookkeeper." Angie put out her hand, smiling in a sultry way that made Tanner lift a knowing eyebrow. "Johann Sebastian Block, jazz musician." J.S. nodded watchfully, not offering a hand, and Tanner inclined his own head with dignity. "Edith Reber, librarian." Edith blushed and looked away. Tanner began to look bored. "You've met my mother, Elizabeth Merrill, and these are my sons, Jamie and Brendan."

"Your sons." Tanner squatted down in front of the boys, who stared solemnly back at him. "They're adorable. I can see Danny in them."

Phoebe tensed. "No doubt." She didn't want to discuss Danny. "Mom, would you take care of these?" She thrust the roses into her mother's arms. Elizabeth looked harassed, probably thinking of the overflowing vases everywhere. "Hadn't we better be going?"

Tanner rose and took her hand. "Of course. Nice to meet you, everyone."

"The pleasure is all ours," Angie gushed. Phoebe pushed Tanner ahead of her out the door.

He opened the door on his side of the car, and not realizing that he wanted her to get in there, Phoebe opened her own door and plopped inside. "You could be sitting closer," he said a trifle testily as she fastened her seat belt. "Who were all those people, anyway?"

Phoebe laid her bag between them on the car seat. The car was big and plush. Somehow its alien interior emphasized the strangeness of the evening. She began to wonder if she was actually awake or not. "Those were my boarders," she said distractedly.

"Boarders!" He looked flabbergasted. "You have to take in boarders?"

"I don't have to," Phoebe said stubbornly. "I like having boarders."

He laughed and reached over for her hand. "Phoebe, you're just as original as ever."

She tried to pull her hand away. "Tanner, drive with both hands, please. I'm looking forward to dinner too much to cope with an accident."

He laughed again. "Don't you know I'm an expert driver?" His voice was caressing, but he did let go of her hand. "I was trained to do my own stunts in the show."

By asking him questions about Hollywood—how he'd gotten his chance at stardom, what it took to do the show—she managed to get through the drive downtown to the fancy restaurant he'd chosen. And there Monk's predictions began to go wrong.

The restaurant was expensive. She knew that because numerous reviews of it in the local papers had bemoaned the incredible prices charged for one perfect lamb chop accompanied by a carved turnip. It was also brightly lit, and noise bounced off the sleek blond-wood and white-lacquer surfaces. The room was buzzing with sound as well-heeled diners tried to communicate with their dates.

Moments after she and Tanner appeared at the door, Tanner was being mobbed by what seemed to be every woman in the restaurant as well as by a good portion of the men. His handsome, confident smile varied not one iota as the clamor around them increased. He signed everything that was thrust at him, including a pair of dainty underpants. Phoebe stood by, looking on while the sensation of unreality deepened.

The maître d' at last succeeded in shooing the patrons back to their own tables. Phoebe allowed him to pull out her chair at the window table, and she sipped from the crystal water glass while Tanner consulted with an endless stream of black-coated men. He ordered for both of them, which she would have resented if she hadn't been struck speechless by the prices on the menu.

When the maître d', the sommelier and the waiter all finished figuratively licking Tanner's boots and went away, there was silence for a moment. Phoebe played with her water glass, waiting for Tanner to speak. She would have enjoyed looking around the dining room at the upper classes, but everywhere she glanced, people were watching them, whispering behind their hands, even waving to get Tanner's attention. It was like the archetypal nightmare where the dreamer is naked and surrounded by gaping people.

"Is it like this everywhere you go?" She looked at Tanner, trying to ignore the people who were staring avidly from the table behind him.

"Pretty much." He shrugged. "I've gotten used to it. Of course, in Los Angeles there are so many celebrities around that people are more blasé about seeing them. I guess I must be the biggest thing to hit St. Louis since the 1904 World's Fair."

Phoebe bridled. It was easy to make fun of St. Louis, but she liked the city and its proud heritage that dated back to the beginnings of the fur trade. "Not at all," she said crisply. "We don't bother our own celebrities, like

Stan Musial and Vincent Price. By the time you're finished filming, you'll probably be old hat."

Tanner looked at her blankly and finally started laughing. "Bee, darling," he gasped, grabbing her hand, "that's why I wanted to see you. That's what I need—your down-to-earth view of things. I've been flattered and catered to for so long I don't know how to act like a normal man."

The waiter brought their appetizers and a bottle of wine and fluttered around them, all but spoon-feeding the catfish mousse into their mouths. Exasperated, Phoebe finally told him they could manage. Before he left, he pulled a folded piece of paper from his tuxedo jacket and handed it to Tanner.

Tanner glanced at it and tucked it into his pocket. "Nothing important," he told Phoebe.

"Does she want to meet you after dinner?" Rattled by the unnerving scrutiny of a roomful of well-dressed people, Phoebe was beginning to lose control of her tongue. To her surprise, Tanner turned a dull red. That was a characteristic of his from the old days, to change color when a sensitive nerve was hit. It made Phoebe feel that somewhere beneath the sophisticated veneer the old Tanner might still exist.

"I can't help it, Bee." Again he took her hand, leaning toward her earnestly. "It's not me, really, it's the TV persona. But since the fact that women find me attractive is good PR, the network keeps building it up. It's out of hand, I know, but if I didn't try to grin and bear it, I'd go crazy."

His fingers massaged the palm of her hand, and his eyes looked deeply into hers. *Here it comes,* she thought, waiting to feel the instant quivering awareness that Monk's touch brought.

But with Tanner's touch—nothing.

"Bee, darling, I've needed to see you. I've been thinking about you for ages—how honest you were and how straightforward. When I found out we were filming in St. Louis this summer, I felt like a dream had come true."

Phoebe dropped her eyes and withdrew her hand. She'd expected this and was even waiting for it, but now she didn't want to hear it. It was one thing to have dinner with an old friend from college days—one who'd become too famous to pass up an opportunity of seeing. It was another thing to endure hints of an intimacy that was suddenly unthinkable.

Hoping to divert him to another topic, she smiled brightly. "Do you remember the first time we met? You dropped your plate practically at my feet and got hamburger and fries everywhere." She savored the last bite of the mousse and added, "I had never heard of eating french fries with gravy before."

Tanner laughed uneasily. "An adolescent whim."

"Not at all," Phoebe said earnestly. "I've noticed since then that people from southern Missouri are more prone to put gravy on any kind of potato, fried or not."

"Well," Tanner said with a hearty laugh, easing his collar away from his neck, "it's certainly not the memory of me that I'd hoped would stick with you." The waiter removed their plates and substituted the entrée—small plump birds in a pool of unlikely-looking sauce. The birds were accompanied by baby vegetables—a tiny ear of corn, a carrot, a turnip. With a flourish of knives the waiter disjointed the birds, and Phoebe saw with horror that the flesh inside was still pink and raw-looking.

"Perfect," Tanner said enthusiastically. "I didn't know anyone outside of Ma Maison knew how to do squab the right way."

Phoebe sat with her eyes fixed on Tanner, watching him pick up the little bones of the squab and suck the meat off them. "Squab—isn't that like baby pigeons?"

"Specially raised to be tender." Tanner noticed that she wasn't eating. "Don't you like it?"

"I've never had it before." Phoebe stuck her fork through the tiny carrot. "Actually, I don't care for rare poultry."

Tanner had evidently become a gourmet. "You haven't lived until you've had duck as it's done at Wolfgang's," he said expansively, refilling his wineglass and hers, although hers was missing only a couple of sips. "They roast the breast separately and—"

"Sure a long way from french fries and gravy." Phoebe didn't want to hear any stories about how to prepare food so it would be raw when it was time to eat.

Tanner winced. "Listen, Phoebe, I'd appreciate it if you'd just forget about the gravy," he said in a low tone, looking around to see if they were being overheard. "I've learned a lot about how to live since then." He sat back and tossed off his wine. "As I recall, you had some pretensions of being a good cook. Haven't you had your food consciousness raised?"

"I just cook regular food with a lot of care," Phoebe said, shaking her head. The waiter came by and deposited another note, which Tanner stuck inside his jacket without reading.

"I remember that first meal you fixed for me," he said huskily. "You came up to my apartment and made spaghetti. We listened to Dylan and made love all night."

Phoebe cleared her throat. "Well, I was living in the dorm, so it couldn't have been all night. I . . . I needed a kitchen to make spaghetti sauce and yours was handy." She frowned at Tanner. "There were three other people there for dinner, as I recall."

"Yes, but they left." Tanner waved his hand impatiently as the waiter removed the entrée plates and served them salad. The greens were really purple and pink instead of green, but Phoebe dived into it hungrily. "Bee, darling, I get the feeling that you don't want me to set a romantic mood tonight."

"Well, actually," Phoebe said, her mouth full of salad, "you're right." She chewed and swallowed. "I know you've been sending me all those unnecessary roses but—"

"Unnecessary!" Tanner's eyebrows went up.

"We ran out of vases after the third batch," Phoebe explained. "You're real popular with the local nursing home." She gulped some of her wine and decided to blurt it all out. "I don't want a romantic entanglement with you, Tanner. You're only going to be here a couple of months—"

"I want you to come back with me," he interrupted her. "I've already made plans. I need you with me, Bee."

"Well, it's no use making plans before you talk with the 'planee,'" Phoebe said indignantly. "I have no intention of going to California. My house is here, my family is here, and my job is here. You don't have anything to offer me that will take the place of those things."

Tanner threw his napkin on the table. "Don't be ridiculous, Bee. I have . . . well, you name it, I have it!" His eyes narrowed as he stared across the table at her. "There's someone else, isn't there? I thought a woman like you would be either married or unattached—you don't take too well to fooling around with no commitment."

"Really, Tanner, it's not—"

"But I guess I had you wrong, huh? You're carrying on with some other guy, and yet you let me send you flowers and sweet-talk you on the phone. You're no better than they are, after all." He took the notes out of his pocket and cast them onto the table with a contemptuous gesture.

Phoebe looked from the notes to Tanner. It was true, really. She had known from the first time Monk kissed her that she loved him. She hadn't wanted to admit it, but she'd known it. And if she loved Monk, what was she doing in a place like this with a man who might never care for any woman as much as he did for himself?

She stood up, pushing her chair away from the table. "You're probably right, Tanner. I'd better go. I don't think we have anything more to say to each other." She picked up her purse and marched between the tables to the door.

She could hear the rising whispers in her wake, but she was too upset to care. She was angry with Tanner, who hadn't changed at all unless to grow more conceited, and angry with herself for being weak enough to go out with him just because he was famous now.

The maître d' flagged down a taxi for her, and she sank into it, reflecting bitterly that even taxicabs were more plentiful near the haunts of those with money. "If he'd become a shoe salesman and called me up for a date, I wouldn't have had to think twice before turning him down," she muttered. It was going to cost her a small fortune to get back to Kirkwood from downtown. Instead of offering to take her home, Tanner was probably salvaging his lady-killer reputation by calling in his notes.

Glumly she looked at the taxi meter. The clock next to it revealed it was only 9:00 P.M. At least the children would be in bed. She dreaded having to explain her stupidity to the audience that had assembled for her triumphal exit such a short time ago.

11

FROM HIS VANTAGE POINT inside the darkened garage, Monk watched Phoebe leave on her date. He had been hoping that she would experience some last-minute qualms. That didn't appear to be happening.

He sighed and switched the light on in the garage. He still had to pack his slack-rope equipment for the show the next day. It had been specially designed to break down into sections that fit into his battered Volkswagen van.

He had long ago figured out the precise method of packing the van so his equipment took up the least amount of space, but tonight he found it hard to concentrate on what he was doing. His mind kept wandering to the scene he'd so bitterly sketched for Phoebe that afternoon. In his imagination he saw the palatial hotel suite, the ice bucket of champagne, the lowered lights, the satin-covered bed....

He shook himself impatiently and finished loading the slack rope, refusing to think about it any more. But when every last piece of equipment was taken care of, all the costumes inventoried and stashed in Angie's car, all the details of the performance arranged, he was hard put to keep from torturing himself further.

Elizabeth had gone off to her room, saying she was too tired to wait up for Phoebe, and the house was silent. He went up to his room to change his sweat-soaked T-shirt for a clean one. Angie was out as usual, J.S. had a gig, and Edith was probably asleep already.

Downstairs the rooms seemed empty without Phoebe's laughter. He paused in front of the little boys' door, head bent, but there was no sound. They were deep in dreamland. There was no crack of light showing under Elizabeth's door, either. He might have invited himself in for a late chat if there had been.

He pushed open the door of Phoebe's room and stood there, not entering, but pleasing himself with the evidence of her presence. The violet fragrance she wore scented the air, and he sniffed it hungrily. Her desk, as usual, was cluttered with piles of paper and file folders, some of them, he knew, pertaining to the work she'd been doing for the troupe.

Considering the short lead time she'd had, she had done an an astounding job of getting articles and hastily taken photos into the local papers. Thanks partly to her work, both shows of the benefit performance were almost sold-out. Their share of the ticket sales would pay expenses and guarantee a generous honorarium to each performer.

He watched the curtains billow in the cool night breeze and fantasized that when he turned she would be waiting for him, her eyes shining as they did when she was particularly moved. But of course there was nothing there when he turned around, and hours would pass before he could expect her back from her date. No matter how ignoble it was and how little befitting one of his knightly lineage, he intended to spy on her return. Not that he would confront her. He just had to know how matters stood between her and the TV goon.

Disconsolately he wandered back outside, drawn by the warmth of the evening and the sweet scent of the mock orange bushes beside the veranda. He sat on the front steps and admired his carpentry work.

The kids had dumped a pile of sand toys beside the steps, no doubt forbidden by their grandma to bring them inside. Monk retrieved a tin cup, a plastic strainer and a funnel from the pile and began to juggle them, trying to divert his gloomy thoughts by tossing behind his back, under his arm—any way he could think of that didn't involve standing up. But the funnel was too light and he kept dropping it. He found it interesting, though, to juggle disparate items so that a pattern emerged, first one thing being tossed all around his body, then the next. Something to do, anyway. He put the toys back and ambled to the garage.

Turning on the light again, he surveyed the interior thoughtfully. He had fixed the roof a few weeks ago so that it didn't leak and sorted through the accumulated rubbish, reducing it substantially. In one corner was some broken lawn furniture he planned on mending. Taking up the back part was a big tractor tire that Phoebe had sheepishly admitted she'd been meaning to make into a sandbox for the past two years.

His love, he thought, looking at the tractor tire, was vague in the puttering-around department. She liked puttering, but without direction she didn't seem to get much done. Just the opposite of how she was at her desk or in the kitchen. Remembering Phoebe in the kitchen that afternoon, he frowned.

"That was a dumb move," he confided to the tractor tire. It had been stupid to quarrel with her after he more or less pushed her into Tanner's arms. In fact, it had been stupid to take the chance of letting her meet the goon in an uncommitted frame of mind. At the time he'd been motivated by pure nobility. Phoebe should confront her choices, not just take him because he was handy and later find herself yearning for the glamour she'd given up.

Now he could only wonder at his crazed behavior. He should have grabbed his woman with as many hands as it took. He should have bound her to him by every tie he could forge, every loyalty he could command. He should have—

"No way, turkey," he muttered to himself. If the same thing were to happen again, he would behave in exactly the same way. He loved Phoebe steadily, needfully, with all the courtliness he was capable of. His love demanded that she must claim him with the same feelings, without a shadow of doubt that it was Merlin Brown she needed and no one else.

He began to whistle a solemn dirgelike tune and to peruse the shelves along one wall, hefting likely-looking bits of junk. A coffee cup without a handle; a pristine plumber's friend, still in its hardware-store bag; a half-used jar of fish fertilizer. He checked that the fish fertilizer lid was screwed on tight and began to juggle, trying different ways to highlight each unlikely item.

His whistling took on a jazz tempo. The rhythm he sought was emerging, but he kept dropping the plumber's friend. Juggling took total concentration, and that was something he couldn't summon this evening. He paused to shake himself all over, willing relaxation, concentration. Then he started again, blocking out everything but the pattern he meant to create.

That was how Phoebe found him when she got back.

She paid the taxi and crept up the front walk, relieved that the house was dark except for a dim light burning in the hall. Perhaps everyone—by "everyone" she meant Monk—was asleep already, despite the fact that it wasn't yet ten o'clock.

Then she saw the light in the garage. Walking toward it, she heard the familiar swish and thud of objects being juggled. The garage door was ajar, and she peeked around it, suddenly shy.

Monk stood in the middle of the garage, under the bare light bulb that hung from the rafters. His face was serious with a slight frown of concentration, and his lips puckered with the mournful, jazzy little tune he whistled. She watched as the plumber's friend came swinging up from behind his back, over his right shoulder, while the cup and the bottle of fish fertilizer circled innocuously. The plumber's friend whizzed between his legs and came back up over his left shoulder.

The scene was very different from the explosive confrontation Phoebe had been dreading during her taxi ride. A crack of nervous laughter escaped her, breaking Monk's concentration.

He dropped everything and spun around, ducking as the plumber's friend narrowly missed his head. The cup bounced harmlessly off the dirt floor, but the bottle of fish fertilizer bounded on top of the cup, and both of them broke.

Distracted, Monk ran his fingers through his hair. "Phoebe..." Fish fertilizer aroma began seeping into the air. "Good grief!"

Phoebe started forward, ready to clean up the broken glass, but Monk shoved her away. "You'll spoil your nice clothes," he began, looking around the garage. Spying an old dish drainer, he worked it under the broken pieces then carried everything out and dumped it into the trash can.

Phoebe trailed after him. Somehow the drama was dissipating. At least the strain was, too. She leaned against the garage door and laughed helplessly.

Monk folded his arms across his chest. "I'm glad you can find something to laugh about in this disaster of an evening," he said sternly.

She could see the smile trying to break through on his mouth. "Why...why the plumber's friend?" she finally managed to gasp.

"It was a challenge," he growled, advancing on her. "Why are you back so early?"

Her laughter died. "It was no challenge at all," she whispered. "I don't know why I should go on dates with someone else, when you're the man I love."

He stood stock-still, caught in the strip of light that streamed from the garage door. He looked vulnerable, open. Phoebe felt her heart swell with love for him. She took a step forward, her hands held out beseechingly. He pulled her toward him slowly until they were clasped in each other's arms.

Phoebe sighed and raised her eyes to his. "I love you," she said again, hoping to see in his expression what she needed and longed to see.

He looked at her, wonder dawning on his face. "Phoebe!" His voice was half-strangled with emotion. "I've been in hell since this afternoon, afraid you wouldn't choose me—"

"There's no choice about it," she said tartly. "Or if there was, I made it weeks ago." She shook him a little. Would he ever say it?

"God, I love you so." He cradled her head in his hands, searching her face, his eyes the clear, intense blue of a flame, so bright she was dazzled and had to blink. All that love, all that feeling...for her! He made a noise deep in his throat and crushed her against him. She looked up at him, starving for his kiss, then closed her eyes again.

Their lips met fiercely in a long, scorching kiss that she wished would never end. She felt delirium invade her body. It was as if she'd never known how much enticement there could be in kissing the man you loved.

They were both trembling when they broke apart, gasping for breath. "Phoebe," Monk said hoarsely. "Sweetheart, I want you so much.... I could...tumble you on that tractor tire...."

Through the turmoil that swirled in her senses, Phoebe managed a chuckle. "How romantic, my lord jester."

He laid his cheek against her hair and held her close for a moment. "I can hardly believe that I'm standing here with you in my arms instead of just dreaming about it." His voice was a low croon in her ear. "I've waited so long to claim you like this, to tell you I love you. . . ."

"Has it been that long?" Phoebe wound her hands dreamily through his hair and trailed her fingers around the delightful curve of his ear. He drew in his breath, and she smiled impishly up at him. "My, what a lot of self-control you have."

"Had," he growled, catching her closer. "My self-control is definitely in the past. Is it to be the tractor tire, woman? Or shall we find something more comfortable?"

Behind the lighthearted words was a wistful appeal that tugged at her heart. Full of love for him, she let her feelings overflow into her eyes, her smile.

She took his hand and led him up the back steps, through the silent, darkened rooms. Pausing inside her room to slip off her shoes, she went to shut the door into the children's room and, after a moment's thought, to snick the bolt across it. Monk turned on the lamp beside her desk, watching her lock the hall door, as well.

"If there's an emergency," she explained, catching his gaze on her, "they can knock. I don't intend to be interrupted tonight."

"So I see." He leaned back against the corner of her desk. "It's a wise precaution. One more cold shower and I'm likely to get hypothermia."

She moved back into the room, filled with an excruciating mixture of shyness and wanton need. As if he divined her mood, Monk caught her hand, stopping her in front of him. The feel of his callused palm, the closeness of his body, caused little shocks of pleasure wherever she touched him.

His eyes were level with hers, looking directly into her with that crystalline gaze. "Feeling nervous, love?"

Reluctantly she nodded. "It's been a long time. I . . . I might be rusty."

Laughter sparkled in his eyes. "I believe it's like riding a horse." He lifted his hand and let one finger trace the outline of her lips. "Once you learn how—" She sucked his finger into her mouth, surprising even herself, and nibbled gently on it. His voice thickened. "You always know...ah, love..." She pressed his hard palm against her mouth and let her tongue trace lazy patterns on it. The sound of his breathing intensified. "You don't seem rusty to me."

The hoarseness in his voice had a strange effect on her knees. She had to lean on him, and his arms came around her, taking quick advantage of her weakness. "I want to make love with you," he whispered, his tongue flicking along her upper lip before he covered her mouth with the hot sweet fire of his. She pressed closer to him, feeling the hard bulge against her thigh with rising anticipation. Her shyness fled as Monk's hands trailed flames along her back. She let her own hands play wantonly with his thick plush hair and the strong column of his neck.

His tongue engaged hers in heated love play while his hands swept up her sides and were poised at last just below the swell of her breasts. The ragged breath she needed pushed her straining nipples against the thin fabric of her blouse. When his fingers found the swollen buds, she gasped again. She craved his touch, but her skin felt flushed and sensitive, needing the cool brush of air, the gentle lave of his tongue. . . . He unfastened the first buttons of her blouse, and she moaned and swayed again, clutching his shoulders tightly.

His indrawn breath when he pushed her blouse off her shoulders was intoxicating. In another moment her bra was off, and he was gazing at her with heavy-lidded eyes. "Beautiful," he breathed, touching the dark nipples gently. He cupped the ripeness of her breasts in both hands, closing his eyes as he brought his mouth first to one peak then the the other in the softest and most maddening of kisses.

"Monk!" Phoebe moaned, trying to press herself closer to him. "Please . . ."

Eyes still closed, he nuzzled his face between the soft mounds he held. "What is it, love? Too fast?"

"Too slow!" Phoebe pulled his face up to hers. She pressed her mouth demandingly to his, invading it with her tongue, kindling a dark, honeyed wildness that swept through her overheated body and brought pulsing awareness to every inch of her. There was an aching necessity within her, aching for the fulfillment only Monk could give her. Deliberately she dropped one hand to his thigh and slid it upward until she felt the bursting life in his loins.

He straightened suddenly, his hands dropping to the side fastener of her skirt, while she fumbled eagerly with his belt. At last they were naked, and then Monk set her gently on the quilt and knelt beside her. "I've wanted so often to pleasure you," he whispered, running his hands over her waist and down her hip to tangle in the dusky curls that hid her womanhood. Phoebe moaned incoherently and arched to meet him. "I've dreamed of lingering here, and here—" he touched her breasts and between her thighs "—but love, I want you so badly I can't wait. I can't take it slow. Are you . . . ready?"

"Can't you tell?" She writhed against him, inviting his touch. "Oh, Monk . . ."

He slid down beside her, one leg anchoring hers open, his fingers finding the bud of pleasure, the slick passage that invited his probing. Phoebe trembled when he lowered his head and sucked her pleading nipples. With her hand she found the heavy weight of his need, and she wanted to feel all of him inside her. "Please, Monk—now!"

"I . . . don't want to . . . hurt you," he panted, raising himself over her.

Impatiently she grasped him, showing him where she wanted him to be. "No more waiting," she said huskily. "Love me, please!"

"The pleasure," he breathed, easing into her, "is all . . . mine. Phoebe, love . . . all around me . . ."

She nestled against him, wanting everything he had to give, unwilling to lose any of the heavy delight that coursed through her. For an endless moment of intense feeling they gazed into each other's eyes, their love and passion spiraling.

Then he moved, and she answered with thrust and parry, faster and hotter, his hands branding her with incendiary touches till she lost conscious thought and was possessed only with a growing pleasure that was almost pain. His hands held her, turned her, increasing the exquisite sensations, and his mouth was his hands' accomplice in bringing her feverish body up, up, until at last release shot through her, as though every bit of her had suddenly achieved blissful weightlessness.

He still held her tightly when she opened her eyes. She gave him a smile of sleepy contentment, pleased to notice the satisfaction on his face.

"Not so rusty, eh?" She stretched languorously and realized he was still buried within her. "Uh, Monk? Were you planning to take up residence?"

"Yes, thank you," he said promptly, as if her question had been an invitation.

"It could be a little inconvenient when we have to get up," she pointed out, flexing herself delicately around him. His response was obvious and gratifying. "Monk, are you—"

"Yes, I am, if you don't mind." He moved against her teasingly, and her sensitized body felt passion flowing back into it. Still joined to her, he pulled her up until she was sitting on his crossed legs, her legs wrapped around his hips. "I'll be slow and gentle this time," he promised, touching her breasts. "I don't want you to get sore."

"Wouldn't think of it," she replied, dazed by the pleasure his searching fingers brought. He dipped one hand between her legs, touching in just the right places to draw languorous sighs from her.

Tenderly they kissed and caressed, the heat building between them slowly but surely. And throughout the short summer night Phoebe's body relearned all the delights of love under Monk's agile tutelage.

"I didn't know this was . . . physically possible."

"Feels good, too, right?"

"I'd say . . . ah . . . so. Where did you . . . ah, Monk!"

"I read the *Kama Sutra* straight through when I was fourteen."

"Mmmm . . precocious. This is the kinkiest thing *I* know how to do."

"Wow! Oh, Phoebe!"

"Isn't it in the *Kama Sutra*?"

"Nooo . . . do it again. . . ."

It was nearly dawn when Monk climbed reluctantly out of bed and pulled his jeans on. "I don't want anybody to freak out by finding me here in the morning," he whispered, gesturing toward the bolted door that led to the boys' room. He tucked the covers around Phoebe's sleepy body. "Sleep late today. Elizabeth said she'd give the kids breakfast."

Phoebe sat bolt upright on the bed. "Monk! The benefit! I totally forgot it. You should have been resting!"

He kissed her forehead and pushed her back down in the bed. "Relax. This was better than sleep, as far as

I'm concerned. I'll get a few hours of very contented sack time, don't worry."

He unlocked the hall door and vanished; moments later Phoebe heard the faint creak of the stairs and the distant click of his door latch. In another minute she was asleep.

12

SHE WAS DREAMING OF DANNY, as she often did; these dreams had ceased to bring her the racking sorrow she'd felt at first, although they left her pensive and mourning for her lost love. But this dream was different. He stood on the bluffs above the Missouri River, a spot they'd often roamed while in college. She had tried to pull him back from the edge, but he'd flashed his reckless grin and taken her hand before leaping far out into the hazy blue sky beyond the bluffs.

Instead of falling as she expected, they soared lazily over the silver loops of the river. "You forget, darlin'," he said with a laugh. "I'm dead. I can't fall."

"Am I dead too?" In her dream she felt no fear, only curiosity.

"Not you, m'dear." He guided them to a landing, and she saw that they stood on the sidewalk before her big old house. "You're alive." She looked up and saw Monk watching them placidly from the doorway of the house. "Go along now."

Then Danny seemed to vanish upward in a swirl of movement, and Phoebe walked up the sidewalk to Monk. She was reaching to clasp his hand when she awoke.

She was clutching her pillow, but a sensation of peace pervaded her being. She would never forget Danny, but she knew from now on her memories of him would be less vital, less longing. "Goodbye, my Danny boy," she crooned into the pillow. Then she raced for the shower to rinse away the few unbidden tears.

Pelted by the warm spray, she felt her mood lighten like bread on the rise. She wanted to sing at the top of her lungs, but it was too early to wake the rest of the household. Instead, she climbed into clean shorts and a T-shirt and headed for the kitchen. If ever a morning cried out for cinnamon rolls, this was it.

She was kneading the dough when Monk came in, blinking sleepily, his running shoes dangling from one hand. He stopped short at the sight of her.

"What are you doing up so early?" The question burst simultaneously from both their throats. Likewise the answer "I couldn't sleep." They laughed, and then he grabbed her for a luxurious squeeze.

"Mmm." His mouth nuzzled into her neck. "You smell so fresh and wonderful. I wanted to be waking up with you today."

"Me, too." She held her doughy hands carefully away from his back, but her lips nibbled along his scratchy chin. "And showering with you, and—"

"Don't say any more, or I might not get to my run." He held her gently away. "What are we making so early in the morning?"

"Cinnamon rolls." She wrinkled her nose at him. "If you'd get out of here I could finish them up."

"Okay, okay. I'll think of them every mile I go." He sat on one of the kitchen chairs to lace up his shoes. Her heart turned over when he yawned and stretched. "I should have slept longer, but I couldn't." He frowned for a moment. "I had the strangest dream. . . ."

"Did you?" She stopped kneading. "So did I."

Their eyes met, but they didn't speak. Then, mindless of the flour on her hands, Phoebe threw herself into his arms. "Monk, I'm frightened." She burrowed her face into his T-shirt. "I love you so much. And I'm afraid I'll lose you. You might go away...you might die! Monk, hold me. . . ."

Monk held her tightly, fiercely, wanting to shield her, knowing it was impossible. "I'm afraid of that, too, love," he said softly. "And I didn't lose someone dear to me, as you did. That's what love is—taking the risk of losing, so you can gain. Would it be better if we didn't love each other?"

She shook her head.

"I'm not going away, you can bet on that," he whispered into her ear. "And I have no plans to die."

"Neither did Danny." Phoebe looked up, her eyes swimming. "Damn, I hate crying over everything like this!" She wiped her eyes on her sleeve. "I know there are no guarantees, Monk. I . . . I just want you to be careful, that's all. You're precious to me."

"The same to you, love." He watched her pull herself together. "Do you think I can go out for my run now if I promise to stay away from trucks and cars?"

Her laugh was watery, but it was there. "Stay away from anything bigger than a breadbasket!" He kissed her once more and left by the back door. "And take your time," she called after him. "The cinnamon rolls won't be done for a while."

Left alone in the kitchen, Phoebe put her dough to rise and got herself a bowl of cereal. While she munched, she struggled to let go of the anxiety that threatened her. For the first few months after Danny's death, she had been obsessed by the boys' health. Every sniffle, every scrape, had seemed to her the ominous forerunner of mortality.

Gradually she had regained her balance. She didn't intend to have it upset by such a wonderful event as falling in love again.

"Act your age, Sullivan," she admonished herself, putting the cereal bowl in the sink. Her well-tuned mother's ear caught the sounds of little people stirring, and she got out the bunny bowl for Brendan and the frog bowl for Jamie. Life was going on all around her. She could jump in or shiver on the shore.

"I'm going to jump," she said aloud as the door burst open. Her sons halted, staring at her.

"I'll jump, too," Jamie decided.

"Me, too!" Brendan demonstrated his jumping ability.

"Okay, you guys!" Phoebe took their hands and jumped with them. "Let's keep the noise down, though. People are sleeping." She looked at her sons' beaming faces. "They have to rest up for the circus," she whispered loudly.

"Circus day! Circus day!" The boys began marching around the table.

By the time Monk finished his run and had a shower, everyone in the house was up. The older ones sat around the kitchen table, bleary-eyed but sipping coffee and sniffing eagerly at the aroma of baking cinnamon rolls. The younger ones had moved their parade to the backyard, where Rufus had assumed the role of chief noisemaker.

Phoebe took the pan of rolls out of the oven and smiled at Monk as he arrived in the doorway. "Just in time." Her voice was husky.

Ignoring the interested bystanders, Monk strolled over to her and put his arms around her. "Looks delicious," he said, letting his eyes rove over her face. "Can I have a sample?"

"Uh-huh." They kissed, tenderly at first, then with more heat. J.S. had to clear his throat twice before they came up for air.

"I win, I win the bet." J.S.'s smile was gleeful.

Angie glared at him. "Okay, you win." She switched her glare to Phoebe. "You just lost me a packet of money. I thought you had more sense than to get involved with a clown."

"No," Phoebe said dreamily, her arms still around Monk's neck. "I don't have more sense. Sorry, Angie."

"I don't know what you're gloating about," Angie told J.S. "It's dimes to dollars we'll be out on our fannies in no time."

J.S.'s face fell. "Phoebe—"

"Have a cinnamon roll." Phoebe put the pan on the table and began serving the rolls, hoping to derail the conversation. She hadn't had time to think about the future of the rooming house, and she didn't want to discuss it with Monk in front of everyone else.

Her ploy worked long enough for her to slip away, closely followed by Monk. "Where can we hide?" His voice was a conspiratorial whisper.

"Up here." She led him up to the second floor and pulled down the folding stairs that provided access to the attic. He followed her dubiously then helped her pull the rickety steps up behind them.

"Can we get out again?" The attic was a stuffy, dusty expanse of boxes and bundles, dimly lit from the grimy windows at each end.

"Not until I say so," Phoebe whispered. "Now we'll have to be quiet and lie low." She hunted around until she found an old mattress set. "The perfect place!"

"I especially like the part about lying low," he murmured, following her down. "But let's not be too quiet. I thought we might tell each other the story of our lives. This seems an appropriate moment in our courtship for that, don't you think?"

She slipped her hand under his T-shirt and stroked the lithe muscles of his chest. "If you really want to talk . . ."

He sucked in his breath. "Maybe later . . ."

PHOEBE TOOK a quick peek through the curtains at the back of the performance area to scan the audience. The Children's Health Association had really done themselves proud. Their usual open-air tent, erected on the spacious tree-shaded lawns of Webster University, had ranks of crowded bleachers marching down from the brightly colored canvas sides, and a clear space just in front of the ring was full of children.

J.S. and his cohorts were readying their instruments for the overture. Elizabeth was near the entrance flap, briskly hawking Laughs Unlimited T-shirts, a last-minute brain wave that was raking in the bucks.

Behind the tent flap that hid the backstage area, confusion reigned. The country-western band and the stand-up comedian preceding the troupe were finished with their acts, but they lingered in fascination, riveted by the over-eager gorillas who were already in their suits. Angie in her spectacular leotard flirted saucily with the leader of the country-western band, and the comedian had joined the jugglers in their warm-up exercises with clubs and balls. Cynthia O'Neill was practicing her reverse three-step in one corner. Phoebe turned away from the peephole and took her place among the jugglers. She was rigid with nerves.

"I've been in plays before," she grumbled to Laura, "and been afraid of screwing up my lines. But this is a thousand times worse. Think of dropping juggling balls out there in front of all those people."

"Just accept the fact that you'll drop one." Laura was cold comfort. "Everyone does sometime. It's not a disaster. You don't have to be perfect, just try to be."

They stood in a loose circle, everyone silent in concentration, juggling to Monk's quietly spoken commands. "Three balls. Four balls. Trade right. Trade left." Automatically Phoebe began to concentrate, tuning out everything but the movements of her hands, and she relaxed by degrees. Soon the jugglers were moving together more precisely in response to Monk's calls.

The comedian shook his head in appreciation. "You guys really have it together." He moved out of the circle,, and at his words Phoebe promptly dropped a ball. Recovering it nicely, she rejoined the juggling to Laura's approving smile.

The fanfare sounded, announcing the opening parade, and they lined up, grabbing handfuls of confetti. Elizabeth had come around to take care of loosing the balloons. The show was about to begin.

The first half-hour passed in a blur for Phoebe. She knew where to stand and what to do, thanks to the constant drilling Monk had put them through. But she did it all in a kind of numb daze, afraid to risk noticing anything for fear of destroying her focus.

At last she loosened up enough to notice her sons staring at her with awed expressions. They had been consigned into Elaine's care when Monk's sister had briefly visited backstage after her arrival. Now they sat between Elaine and a string of older kids who must be Monk's nieces and nephews. Phoebe winked at her sons and resolutely turned her attention away before she'd get distracted.

The show was going well, with lots of cheering and laughing from the audience. Monk had invited a kid from the front row to join him and was cleverly making it appear that the boy was juggling instead of the awkward mime behind him. Phoebe was for the moment in the background, waiting for the finale. Her gaze wandered over the crowd again and then she gasped, her eyes widening.

Standing in the entrance to the tent, already attracting the attention of nearby women, was Tanner.

Gabbling a hasty explanation to Laura, Phoebe slipped out the stage entrance and hurried around the outside of the tent. How Tanner could have found out her whereabouts was second place in her thoughts. Uppermost was resentment at him for coming, for butting in where he wasn't wanted.

Tanner still stood at the door to the tent, smiling graciously around at his fans. Already the spectators were turning their attention from the stage to the door, whispering and craning to see what was happening.

Phoebe lunged for his arm and propelled him out of the tent before he knew what hit him. She whispered to the awestruck ticket taker, "Keep people in their seats!" and pulled her captive around to the backstage area where none of his fans would see him.

The area was deserted, and she stood amid a welter of gorilla costumes, glaring at him with her hands on her hips. "That was a low-down trick." She kept her voice subdued, but it fairly trembled with outrage. "Do you always horn in on other people's territory?"

Tanner scratched his head. "I was just looking for you," he said in an injured voice. "Can I help it if people recognize me everywhere I go?"

"Oh, butter wouldn't melt in *your* mouth, I know," Phoebe said in exasperation. She looked around and caught up a gorilla head and clapped it over him while he stood gaping at her. "There. Now you can find out what it feels like to be one of the unrecognized masses."

"Phoebe! This is outrageous!" Tanner's words were slightly muffled by the gorilla head, and Phoebe was struck with a wild desire to giggle. The troupe began to stream backstage to change for the finale. Everyone shot puzzled looks at Phoebe's coercing a stranger into a gorilla suit, everyone but Angie, who took one look and knew who it had to be.

She opened her mouth for a pleased shriek, but shut it again when she caught Phoebe's militant eye. Dancing over to the imprisoned Tanner, Angie cooed, "Mr. Hayden—Tanner—I'm *such* a fan of yours! I didn't know you'd be appearing with us today!"

Inarticulate sounds of protest came from the gorilla mask, but Phoebe ruthlessly ignored them. She pushed Tanner into the rest of the suit and zipped it with businesslike movements.

"There." She stood off and looked at him for a moment then put his hairy paw in Angie's. "You do just what Angie does and you'll be all right. If you're good, I'll let you make a pitch for the Children's Health Association after the show."

Ignoring his incoherent protest, Phoebe hurried over to Monk, who was cramming on his deerstalker in preparation for the beginning of his skit. "Tanner's here," she began hurriedly, not wanting it to be a surprise to him. "He—"

"Tanner's here?" Monk's eyebrows drew together. "What's he want?"

Phoebe shrugged. "I don't know. I don't know how he knew where to look, either." But when she glanced over at Angie, who held her gorilla mask in her hand while she cooed up at Tanner, she had a sudden flash about where the information had come from. Angie had pumped Phoebe earlier about her date. The name of Tanner's hotel had come up in the conversation.

"He's here, anyway," she continued briskly, trying to ignore Monk's scowl. "And we might as well put him to good use. I thought Gloria would like it if he came on after the show and put in a pitch for donations. Maybe he'll ante up himself, who knows?" She grasped Monk's arm urgently. "Monk, don't you see? It doesn't matter what brought Tanner here. I made my choice last night—long before last night. You're the only man who has the power to move me now."

The scowl faded from Monk's face, though the glance he threw Tanner was far from friendly. "How can I blame him for running after you?" His voice was rueful. "After all, I've been making a career of it lately. All right, all right, I'll give the poor sap my sympathy."

While the final skit started onstage, Phoebe hunted up Gloria Taylor, who was enthralled to think that Tanner Hayden would be soliciting funds at her benefit. She thanked Phoebe profusely and as an afterthought introduced her to another woman who stood there. "This is Jean Carpenter from the West County Preschool Coalition. They're planning a fund-raiser, and she's been asking me about your troupe. Excuse me, please. I must tell Helen the good news."

Explaining to Mrs. Carpenter that she had to get backstage, Phoebe scrawled her name and phone number on a card and hurried away. She barely had time to climb into her suit before the music cue. There would be time to rejoice over Monk's good fortune later.

Angie had taken her job of leading Tanner seriously. Phoebe saw her guiding him through the backstage flaps as she finished frantically zipping herself into her own costume. The little boys were not joining them onstage, having been judged unready for the big time, so Phoebe expected the dancing-gorillas section of the show to go smoothly this time.

Instead it was a nightmare. It seemed that Tanner, star of the small screen, had two left feet.

In vain did Angie attempt to guide him through the simple steps of the dance routine. His gorilla mask had been knocked crooked at some point, and now his head swung around in confusion. "Sorry," he muttered as he crushed Phoebe's toes. "I can't see a thing in here!" He careered off her and smacked into Ross, bypassing the swipe Angie made at him.

The rest of the troupe tried manfully to keep their positions, without much success. The dance began to resemble a football scrimmage, with everyone trying to avoid the blind rampages of Tanner.

At last Phoebe and Angie made a determined advance on him, crossed his arms and grabbed his hands in a kind of frontal straitjacket. "Left *kick*, right *kick*," Phoebe said in a hissing whisper through her gorilla mask. Angie reached up unobtrusively and straightened the head so that Tanner could see out.

At once he calmed down and began following along. "I'm going to get you for this, Bee," he muttered.

The music reached a crescendo, and the gorillas moved forward to line up with everyone else and bow. The wild applause went to Phoebe's head like wine. She laughed.

"Upset because I made a monkey out of you?" The troupe filed out the back tent flap, and she pulled the head off her costume. "You were a great gorilla. Probably the best part you'll ever get. Here." His name was being announced by an excited Gloria Taylor, and Phoebe reached up to take off Tanner's gorilla head before she pushed him back through the flap. "It's the county Children's Health Association, and donations are welcome."

Angie crowded up to the flap to watch the audience lose their cool over Tanner, but Phoebe turned away. She had all the excitement she needed in the form of one sexy monkey who was going to be hers forever—or she'd know the reason why.

Monk was being mobbed in one corner. Phoebe got close enough to guess that it was his family, including several kids, Elaine and Lance with spouses, and Guinevere Brown with a stocky, gray-haired man who must be Monk's father. Uncertain, she began to slip away.

Monk saw her and called out, "Phoebe! Over here!" He reached to pull her close when she approached. "Great show, sweetheart." He kissed her, a light but hungry touch on the lips, and tucked her beside him.

"This is Phoebe Sullivan, landlady, juggler and one-woman advertising agency. My dad, Rosemary, Ted." He waved an inclusive hand. "You've already met the rest of the adults, and the kids are too rowdy to introduce." A clamorous protest greeted this statement, with Phoebe's two joining in as though they'd known Monk's nieces and nephews for ages instead of two hours.

Phoebe smiled shakily at everyone. The excitement of the performance still roiled through her, and meeting Monk's family en masse was not helping to settle her stomach. Still, it had to come some time.

Monk's father was beaming. "You've really pulled a nice show together," he said, pumping Monk's free arm. "Didn't think you had it in you, boy."

"Yes, very amusing," Lance added, smiling affectionately at his younger brother. "But Monk—Merlin," he corrected himself at a cough from his mother, "it can't possibly pay you enough to support a—"

"Never mind that now," Elaine broke in, glancing uneasily at Phoebe. "This is a celebration, not a post-mortem."

"Speaking of celebrations," Phoebe spoke up, "the party's laid on at my place. We'd like you all to come by after the second show."

"Sounds like fun." Monk's father gave a parting shake to his arm. "We can talk there."

TO PHOEBE, wending her way through the living room with a fresh assortment of cheeses, it didn't seem that anyone would be able to talk over the din that filled the house. All the troupe members had invited friends and relatives to celebrate. Even Edith proudly introduced a fellow librarian whose pleasant brown eyes blinked dazedly behind thick-lensed glasses. Evidently he was overcome by Edith's transformation from mouse to—well, not lioness, but certainly pussycat.

The Brown contingent was split, with the older folks chatting in the living room and the kids playing some complicated game in the backyard with half the neighborhood. Even Monk's mother seemed to have got into the spirit of the thing. Perhaps the three paper cups of jug wine she'd quickly downed when she'd arrived at the party had something to do with it. Now she was standing next to the piano, belting out a passable "Night and Day," with J.S. tickling the ivories in his best Cole Porter style.

Phoebe set the tray down on the library table and scanned the crowd for Monk. She didn't see his father anywhere, either, though Rosemary and Ted were engrossed in a discussion with Phoebe's mother that ended with Elizabeth taking them out the front door to point at something in the trees.

Tanner was the center of a group in the dining room, where Angie and several of the neighbors hung breathlessly on his description of shooting an episode of his TV show in the Ecuadorian jungle. But it was clear to Phoebe that he was bored, and she wasn't surprised when with Angie clinging to his arm he made his way over to her to say goodbye.

"Angie and I thought we'd go out for a bite to eat," he told Phoebe, edging toward the door. "She knows some places to go later that might amuse me."

"Have a good time." Phoebe's lips quirked, but she fought to set a guard on her tongue.

"Bee, darling, did you really mean what you said last night?" Dropping Angie for a moment, he pitched his voice only for her ears. "Because . . . you've changed, sweetheart. I see that now." His eyes dropped momentarily to the contours of her body that were defined by the shirt and denim skirt she wore. "In very attractive ways. Are you sure we can't . . . well, recapture the rapture?"

Phoebe couldn't help the sputter of laughter that escaped her. "Tanner, Tanner," she said, patting his arm. "It wasn't really rapture to begin with, you know. I'm glad to renew your acquaintance, but I'm not interested in romance. Not with you, anyway." She saw Monk and his dad come down the stairs, and her eyes lingered on them involuntarily.

Tanner saw the direction of her gaze. "So that's the way the wind blows," he muttered. "You prefer that—that clown to me. Very well, my dear. *Hasta mañana*, as we say in California." He took Angie's arm again and marched out the door.

Other people were beginning to leave, as well: Phoebe stood by the door, saying farewell as Edith went out with her librarian; J.S. swirled away for downtown festivities; the neighbors went home to start supper. Finally it was just her family and Monk's remaining.

The living room was littered with paper napkins, half-filled cups, empty soft-drink cans and a few squashy pieces of cheese. Elaine was already taking a plastic bag around to collect debris, with Rufus's enthusiastic help in the matter of cheese disposal.

"Sit down, dear." Guinevere Brown collapsed onto the sofa herself, pushing her silver-frosted bangs off her forehead. "Ooo, I think I had too much to drink. But that young man played so divinely—Tommy, we must engage him to play the next time we have a party. He lives here, does he?"

"J.S.? Oh, yes, he has a room upstairs." Phoebe's reply was absent. Monk and his dad were in the kitchen, and she discreetly craned her neck to see what they were doing. "Oh, Elaine, you don't have to do that!"

"It's all done, anyway." Elaine pushed the bag of trash into the kitchen and perched on one corner of the library table. "I should think you'd be exhausted, Phoebe. You guys sure put on a good show."

"Yes, I was pleasantly surprised," Guinevere allowed. "I never realized Merlin was such a good performer. So clever of him."

Monk came back in with his dad, followed by the children. Jamie and Brendan climbed onto Phoebe's lap. "Uncle Monk said I could be in the show next year!" Jamie cried. "Brendan can't be in it till he's six, but I can be in next year."

"Lucky you." Phoebe hugged her sons, knowing it wouldn't be long before Jamie would be too big for such caresses. She wondered how they would react to a long-term relationship with Monk.

"Bathtime," Elizabeth said from the doorway. But Monk's father stopped her.

"Just a moment, Mrs. Merrill—Elizabeth, if I can call you that. I wanted to propose a toast." Elaine passed out fresh cups to everyone while Monk worked the cork out of a bottle of Piper Sonoma, resplendent in its gilt paper. "Merlin and I have been talking over an arrangement that I think will greatly benefit both of us." He waited until everyone's cup had been filled and then raised his own. "To our new executive vice president for corporate strategy!"

Phoebe sat stunned while around her Monk's family enthusiastically repeated the toast. Was Monk selling out at last?

He was regarding her with a steady, burning glance, and she kept her bewildered eyes fastened on him while his father went on.

"I had a hard job to persuade Merlin to come back to us, since he is modest about his unique abilities in finance and strategy. But we talked, and at last I agreed that the position I'd outlined to him could be accomplished in less than forty hours a week, fifty weeks a year—given a well-trained staff. So Merlin will be working full time six months a year, beginning in October. He'll work half-time three months, April, May and September and be off June through August, during which time he wants to revert to his alter ego, Monk."

Phoebe smiled at Monk and raised her cup to her lips. It was the strangest-sounding job description she'd ever heard, but Monk evidently wanted to try it, so she would accept it, as well. They could still be together this summer, and maybe by fall something permanent would be worked out between them. Still, the uncertainty made her catch her breath.

"That's all the time I'll take up with business," Monk's father concluded. "I just thought you'd all like to know we've managed to lure our absent wizard back into his fold. And Merlin, I wanted to make one more stipulation about your job—you'll need to find time to hold some juggling workshops for our employees. I hear it's an excellent stress-reduction technique, and I plan to take it up myself." He wiped his forehead and took a swig of champagne. "God knows I could use some stress reduction."

Monk's family smiled delightedly, and conversation became general for a few moments while they got ready to leave. Phoebe saw Monk exchange a nod and a smile with her mother. As soon as his family had left, he turned back to the little boys and knelt in front of them. "Jamie, Brendan, I need to borrow your mother for a while."

Jamie looked at him, puzzled. "What for?"

"Come here, I'll tell you." Monk pulled both the boys close and whispered in their ears.

Phoebe stood with her hands on her hips. "What's going on here, anyway?" She looked accusingly from her mother to the little boys, who all wore the same smug smile. "Some kind of secret conspiracy, is it?"

"If it is, I won't tell," Elizabeth said placidly. "You never could keep a secret." She herded the little boys together. "Tell your mother to have a nice time, and you'll see her later."

"Have a nice time, we'll see you later," the boys chorused dutifully. Monk swept Phoebe out the door, but not before she'd heard Brendan pipe, "Bye, Uncle Daddy."

A few seconds after they'd gone, the crystals on the chandelier tinkled happily in the still evening air.

PHOEBE LOOKED SUSPICIOUSLY at Monk as he pushed her into Elizabeth's compact car. "I haven't got all the stuff out of my van yet," he told her, pulling away from the curb, "so Elizabeth let me borrow her car."

"Where are we going?" They were driving north on Lindbergh Boulevard, but that told Phoebe nothing, since they could be going to the grocery store or the airport in that direction.

"Did you forget we have a date?" He made a show of looking at his watch. "It's not seven yet, but Elizabeth said we could leave early."

"Monk, you have to tell me what's going on."

"Not for a little while," he pleaded, keeping his eyes on the busy Saturday-afternoon traffic. "In fact, maybe I should blindfold you."

"No, no, I won't ask any more questions!"

"Hah!"

"I promise. But I don't understand about this whole thing with Brown Bearings."

"See? Already asking questions."

"That was a statement, not a question."

"Very well, I'll tell you."

And for the next half-hour he talked enthusiastically about the offer his father had made, the new challenges that would be his, the team he'd need to set up, the way his salary would provide for lavish living and still leave money over to establish a funding base for Laughs Unlimited's summer circuit. "We'll start recruiting and retraining the troupe in April, rehearse and develop material until the season starts in June, tour around between St. Louis and Kansas City all summer—maybe even hit Chicago, who knows? Then in the fall when we have to hang up our tights, I'll go back to work full time. Perfect setup, eh?"

Phoebe's attention was distracted as they entered a parking garage in the posh, recently restored West End of St. Louis. "Monk, where are we?"

"Shh," he said, seizing a couple of suitcases from the back seat and steering her to an elevator. "Remember, you weren't going to ask questions."

They traveled in silence until the elevator doors opened on a spacious hotel lobby, elegantly decorated with Persian rugs and crystal chandeliers. Monk gave the suitcases to a bellboy and had a hasty conference with the desk clerk in a voice too low for Phoebe to hear. Then he was back, taking her arm and guiding her into the elevator again.

"Monk," she said warningly. "I think I'm going to burst if I don't get some answers."

He looked down at her, the intense blue of his eyes practically radiating excitement. "Don't worry, honey. It won't be long. And then I'll be the one wanting answers. Or at least one answer."

Phoebe's heart began a slow slam as she took in the significance of his words. She was still pondering them when the bellboy opened a tall, gilt-trimmed door, set the bags inside and discreetly disappeared.

Stepping into the room, she looked around in wonder. The furnishings were as elegant as the lobby had been. Graceful Queen Anne armchairs and a love seat were grouped around a gleaming table, where another bottle of Piper Sonoma reposed in a silver ice bucket next to an ornate basket of fruit. The huge bed, its massive contours draped with satin curtains, was tucked in an alcove. An arrangement of pinecones occupied the immaculate marble fireplace. Through an open door she could glimpse more marble in the bathroom, trimmed with crystal and gold.

"The satin sheets," she whispered, "the champagne in a silver bucket, the flowers . . ." She looked around. "You slipped up, Monk. I don't see any flowers."

"I brought them with me." He reached in his pocket and took out a tiny velvet box. Her heart lurched when he pressed it into her hand. Opening it, she saw a delicate tracery of gold and diamonds in the form of a white violet.

"It was my grandmother's," Monk said huskily, his eyes intent on hers. "My mother brought it with her today, after I told her I was going to ask you to marry me. Will you wear it, Phoebe? Will you marry me?"

She couldn't find words. With trembling fingers she lifted the ring out of the box and slipped it over her finger. It fit perfectly.

"I've already got the boys' consent," he continued anxiously. "And your mother's, too, for what it's worth. She packed your suitcase and agreed to watch the children tonight."

Phoebe looked at the suitcase then back down at the flower that shimmered on her hand. "It's . . . it's beautiful, Monk."

"It suits you, then." He put his arms around her, still tentative. "I love you so much, Phoebe. I've spent the past three months learning to know you and love you. I didn't know there was a woman like you anywhere in the world, and now that our lives have come together, I don't want them to part. Ever."

She lifted her eyes to his, trying to tell him without words how much he stirred her. "Monk—"

"I'm not finished, love." He kissed her gently and went on. "I love your family, your children. They make a perfect new family, although I wouldn't mind adding to it in the future. I love your house, and I even love the boarders, although I don't think we'll need them when I can share expenses with you."

Phoebe blinked away a mist of tears. He was so gentle, so careful of her independence. "Monk—"

"Phoebe, love, will you marry me?"

She launched herself at him and put her hand firmly over his mouth. "Will you let me get a word in edgewise?"

He nodded, his eyes dancing above her hand.

"Will you stop interrupting me every time I try to say something?"

He made a muffled noise she took for assent.

"Well, then, you big ape, I'll marry you."

More noises from behind her hand. "Mmph uhr hmpf humf."

"What?"

He tore her hand away. "I said, take your hand off so I can kiss the dickens out of you."

"Then you have to take your shirt off."

"Then you have to take your skirt off."

Gleefully they disrobed each other, falling at last onto the big satin-covered bed, their laughter dissolving into something much more potent.

"Monk—"

"Don't interrupt me now, darling. I just need to . . ."

"Mmm . . . Monk, we forgot the . . . champagne. . . ."

"Do you need it?"

"I don't know. If there was lots more of it we could put it in that fancy marble tub and bathe in it."

"You talk too much, wife."

"Monk, we could get married in the gorilla suits!"

"Not on your life, my sweet bride-to-be. You're delirious, and I have the cure. . . ."

"Oh, ooh . . . that's it—that's the . . ."

"I love you, Phoebe."

"I love you, my knight in jester's clothes."

"No clothes at all, right now."

"It looks great on you."

Resting later on the satin sheets while Monk splashed champagne into tall fluted glasses, Phoebe regretfully gave up the idea of a circus wedding. "I know," she said suddenly. "I'll bet your mother would like a medieval wedding. Wreaths for our hair, doublet and hose for you . . ."

"Wouldn't I have to wear motley and bells?" He handed her the champagne, and they clicked glasses solemnly. "Here's to my lady, my life."

"Here's to my jester," Phoebe whispered, drowning in his eyes. "My love forever."

This month's
irresistible novels from

—TEMPTATION—

THE RIGHT TOUCH by Eileen Nauman

As a TV camera operator and competing fencer, Devorah Hunter had enough to handle. She didn't need a tough, sexy guy like Cal Travis around – she suspected he was a real lady-killer.

Yet when she met the notorious pilot at an embassy party in Hong Kong, she was in for some surprises. Devorah had planned on keeping her distance, but somehow her plans and Cal's moves just kept pulling them closer and closer . . .

WITHOUT PRECEDENT by JoAnn Ross

Quinn Masterson was established, successful – and looking for a wife. When Jessica O'Neill entered the picture, he knew she was the one. But how to prove that to the gorgeous fellow attorney and mother of three?

The relationship was already hampered by the fact that he and Jessica were on opposite sides of a divorce case. And though she obviously enjoyed his searing kisses, she no longer believed in happily-ever-afters. Quinn would have to employ his most persuasive arguments . . .

HEAD OVER HEELS by Leigh Roberts

Phoebe Sullivan managed to fill every nook and cranny of her old boardinghouse with muddy kids, offbeat roomers and warm smells from the oven. But when the irresistibly charming Monk Brown came to stay, she found her well-ordered life turned into a juggling act.

Monk's constant presence was a sensually charged distraction. The gentle touch of his lips, his electrifying embrace, made her achingly aware. Stolen moments of passion were not enough – she needed more, much more . . .

Spoil yourself next month
with these three novels from

—TEMPTATION—

SOMETHING TO TREASURE by Rita Clay Estrada
(Final novel in this author's trilogy)

Men! To Brenda Hunt they were all alike – selfish, egocentric boors. And who had time for them, anyway? A single parent, Brenda had three children to raise, a house to run, a job to keep.

Leo Coulter was an especially maddening case – wealthy, devastatingly handsome, completely sure of his own attractiveness. His persistent attentions puzzled Brenda, infuriated her – and awakened a hunger that had been dormant for years . . .

DESIGNING WOMAN by Candace Schuler

Starting an affair with your ex-husband *was* a little unorthodox, Daphne Granger admitted. But she had never stopped loving Adam since their divorce eleven years earlier.

Meeting him now after all this time brought back the memories – and all the old feelings. Daphne saw the hunger in his gaze, felt the desire in his touch . . . and found herself responding. Yes, a simple affair was the answer, she thought. It would get him out of her system for good . . .

AFTER THE RAIN by Madeline Harper

The day, Emma Dixon reflected wearily, had been a disaster. A garbled telegram from her mother had sent her rushing off to the Yucatán. Now Emma was stranded in the middle of the jungle, a fierce storm impending.

Her only way out was with Jack Winston. Tall, virile, handsome, the renowned film-maker was none too pleased with his role of rescuer. Emma would have to use all her wiles to convince him otherwise . . .